FOLLOW THE
WESTWARD
STAR

Historical Western Fiction

GLENDA C MANUS

Author of The Southern Grace Series

Library of Congress Cataloging-in-Publication
Data is on file with the publisher

Text copyright © 2020 by Glenda Manus
Published in 2020 by South Ridge Press
ISBN-13: 978-1-7326710-3-4

Printed in the US
Interior Design by Diane Turpin Designs
Cover Design by South Ridge Designs
Edited by Dorothy Pennachio
Content Editor: Lee Cook

First Original Edition

This novel's story and characters are fictitious. Certain historical landmarks and
notable people of the time period are mentioned but the characters involved are
wholly imaginary.

South Ridge Press
949 Wilson Dr.
Lancaster, SC 29744

FOREWORD

"What?" you must be asking. "Where is Book 9 in the Southern Grace Series with Rev Rock, Liz, and Matthew? Why are we not dropping in to share a glass of sweet iced tea with our neighbors in the charming little village of Park Place, South Carolina? Where is Maura, Holly, Reva, Agatha, May, and postmistress Betty? Oh, and what about Paradise Cove? Will Rock and Liz stay or go?"

Don't worry! Hang in there with me a little longer. Book 9 is coming soon, I promise!

Speaking of promises, my husband is a fan of novels about the Old West and he has asked me many times to write a book in the Western Historical Fiction genre. The talented Louis L'Amour (may he rest in peace) is my husband's favorite western author and since I am also a big fan of the late Mr. L'Amour, I promised him I would give it a try. I had not planned to start quite yet, but life's circumstances spurred me on.

You see, this past winter my husband was diagnosed with a medical condition that made us rethink our mortality. It made me realize if I was going to fulfill my promise to write a Western for him, I should not dilly-dally around. Thanks to the power of prayer, he has recovered nicely and is looking forward to reading *Follow the Westward Star*. I sincerely hope that you, my dear readers, will enjoy it as well!

Thank you for supporting me in my endeavor to write in a different genre! You're the best!

~~~Glenda Manus~~~

CHAPTER ONE
KENTUCKY 1851

The dishes had been cleared from the kitchen table and the tantalizing smell of freshly-baked cherry cobbler hung in the air. Words, like a tattered sheet on a clothesline, also hung in the air from the letter Rafe McCade had just read to his wife and thirteen-year-old son. The letter was something to ponder upon.

It was a letter from his brother, Colin—a letter so tattered that it looked to have been read a hundred times already. It wasn't unusual for letters to arrive that way, especially letters that had traveled all the way east from the western territories by stagecoach, steamboat, and occasionally in the saddlebag of a lone rider. And it wasn't unusual for one to have been read a few times along the way—hastily torn open to hear news from the men and women who were daring enough to move west—and then gently pasted back together so the letter could be sent on to the intended recipient. It may have first been opened by the hands of a station master at a lonely relay station waiting for the arrival of the next stagecoach or read by the smoke-filled eyes of a cowhand by a campfire who had been asked to deliver it to the next post on his route back from a cattle drive.

It was only the fourth letter Rafe had received from either of his brothers since they'd gone west two years before. Colin and Ennis were the second and third in line out of the five McCade boys and they were the most adventurous of the lot. When their Pa died, there was no reason for them to stay on the Kentucky farm, so they had gone west.

Rafe's wife, Dora, sat at the table with him and was drumming her fingers on the tabletop impatiently. "Go on, read the rest of the letter."

"That's all there is to it," he said, looking sideways at her.

"That ain't so," she said. "There's more writin' on that page."

Still teasing, Rafe sniffed the air. "That cobbler is mighty temptin'. Can't we just dip into it first?"

Dora's fingers started drumming even harder and the look she gave him was scathing. "Rafe McCade, if you don't read the rest of that letter, I'm throwin' that cobbler to the pigs."

He laughed. "We don't have any pigs."

"Then I'll feed it to the birds. They always try to beat me to the cherry tree anyway."

Dora was always eager to hear news from his brothers' western travels and it had been months now since either brother had written. She had been raised in the hills of eastern Tennessee, her family always just scraping by. She'd had no schooling and couldn't read or write, but she made up for it in common sense, and Rafe had learned early to rely on her instincts and her keen sense of judgment.

It was the year of 1851, and a rough winter it had been. If it hadn't been for brother Kirk sharing his harvest, it would have been worse. While Rafe was grateful for the help, he was hell-bent on never letting it happen again. Being the youngest of the boys, his part of the family inheritance had been a few scraggly acres on the east side of his daddy's farm, and his granddaddy's before him. The land was worn out from too many plantings of the same crops year after year and he didn't have enough acreage to let his fields lie fallow to rest between plantings.

There'd been bad blood in the family since their father, Benjamin Furgus McCade had died. The eldest brother Aiden, a bad-tempered and greedy man, had dictated how the estate would be settled, keeping the choicest piece of land for himself and the lowliest for Rafe and Kirk. Old Benjamin kept a firm hand on Aiden while he was living but when he died, Aiden's true nature had shown through.

The letter on the table was from Colin and he was telling Rafe there was land to be had for the taking in the New Mexico Territory. Of all the boys, Colin had been the smartest, and their pa had let him stay in school longer than the others. He looked down at the letter again admiring his brother's handwriting.

"Okay, don't get your dander up," he said and reached out to rest his large bony hand over Dora's small one. "If you'll stop that infernal tapping on the table, I'll read the rest." Her hands went still, and she folded them in her lap as Rafe picked the letter back up and read from where he'd left off.

> *I've taken a wife, a comely widow whose man was killed by Indians north of here. She has a boy who I'm raising as my own, and we'll soon be having another. I'm hoping for another boy, but if it's a girl, she'll be a feisty little German maiden like her mama and that's all that matters. Mira is a good wife and her boy, Lenny, is nigh on six and a quick learner.*

> *We have a fine place here but could use some neighbors. It's in the New Mexico Territory, not long won from Santa Anna.*

Some are beginning to call it Colorado named after the river that slices right through it. I've heard it's the biggest river west of the Mississippi, but I've not seen it myself. We've settled on the North Platte River east of the Rocky Mountains. The area reminds me a little of the Appalachia hills of Tennessee where you met Dora, but instead of hardwood trees, we mostly have ponderosa pine and juniper. The valley is plush and green— like nothing you've ever seen, Rafe. Creeks and streams run through the valley like fingers snaking their way down to the Arkansas River. Full of fish too, and we have enough antelope and buffalo out here to feed and fatten up the whole state of Kentucky. Our cabin is built downstream on Big Sandy Creek.

We'd be glad if you and Dora and your boy would come out here with us—brother Kirk too if he's able, but I'm wagering that his Sarah won't cotton to leaving her Ma behind since she's getting on in years. There's lumber aplenty and we'll build you a cabin and barn in no time. I know our brother Aiden wouldn't come even if I asked, which I won't. Good riddance to him, I say. Brother Ennis went on to California from here, joining a wagon train of men et up with gold fever. It doesn't take much to turn your brother's head, and he being single and all, he packed up and off he went. He says he'll come back when he has a bucket full of gold so we can buy us a herd of cattle. But you know how he is—I'm not depending on it. I've got some strays without a brand on 'em that I've already rounded up. They're offspring from a herd owned by an old man who settled in the valley a few years past. He's dead and gone now as most of the cows are, but there were a few bulls amongst 'em and they've multiplied. They favor the rich grass in our valley and don't wander far.

We've Indians here, mostly Arapaho and Cheyenne. They're right friendly and ain't give us any trouble, and I don't reckon they will as long as we leave em alone. But we dare not travel far to the North where the Sioux are making trouble. It was them that killed Mira's man.

Tell Dora this is a fine place to raise a boy. Your Tom will like it out here and Dora would get along just fine with my Mira. She gets awfully lonely and never sees another woman 'cept when a wagon train comes through the pass south of here. We always hear news of it and there ain't nothin to do but go out and meet 'em and pester 'em to death for news from the east.

Rafe refolded the letter. He'd read it three times already since Kirk delivered it to his doorsteps on his way from town this morning. He had gone immediately to the barn so he could read it without Dora standing over him. There were a few more scribbled words giving some general directions and a crude map drawn of the best-known trails to follow. Each time he reread the letter his excitement grew. This was the first time he'd read it out loud to Dora, and he watched for her reaction. She was on the edge of her seat.

"Let's go, Rafe. We ain't got much here, workin' hard and nothin' to show for it. It would be a fine place to raise Tom."

She was earnest; he could tell. "It would be a hard trip," he said. "If you think life here is hard, you don't know what you're getting yourself into going so far into rough country." At her look of disappointment, he put his hand across the table and took hers. "I promised you when I took you from the hills, I would give you a better life, but here we are, not much better off than your family was. At least we've got a fine stock of horses and a few cattle. And we've got a good farm wagon.

"I'll tell you what—we'll think it through and pray over it. I can't say we will, but I won't rule it out either. Maybe the Lord will make it clear for us."

A warm smile spread across her pretty freckled face. "Fair enough."

"Now, about that cobbler," he said with a smile of his own.

"Comin' right up!" She scurried from the table.

IT WAS A COLDER than normal spring with frost up through the end of April shortening the normal planting season. When the warmth finally arrived, Rafe and Kirk raced to get their corn planted. Kirk was using the ox they owned between them to break up his field, so Rafe walked the path to Aiden's house to ask if he could borrow his ox just for the day. When he didn't find his brother at home, he went to the barn and led the ox back to the field with a rope. He had no sooner hitched the ox to the plow when Aiden came barreling in on his horse.

"Who said you could use my ox for plowing? I got my own garden to break up."

"I didn't think you'd mind, Aiden. You weren't home, so I couldn't very well ask you. I'll be finished by mid-day and bring him back. And anyway, this was Pa's ox. He should belong to all of us."

Aiden's ears turned a bright red, a sign of anger that Rafe knew well. He'd been on the receiving end of that anger quite often and was about to be again as Aiden turned the horse around and almost rammed him in the chest.

Rafe was livid. "Aiden McCade, you treat us like we're your stable servants. You must think you're one of those barons in some fancy estate over in England. You've been looking at Ma's fancy books too much. Pa would turn over in his grave if he could see how you're treating your brothers."

His words hit a nerve with Aiden. It was true and it galled him that Rafe was mocking his perceived image of himself.

"That ox best be in my stable by noon. And don't be borrowing nothing else without asking." He jerked on the horse's reins, ready to start down the path.

"Wait," Rafe called out. As Aiden turned around, Rafe was unhitching the ox from the plow. He handed the lead rope to his brother.

"You can have your old ox," he said. "I won't be laying this ground aside after all. I'm turnin' my share of land over to Kirk and moving to New Mexico Territory with Dora and the boy."

Aiden looked at Rafe in disbelief and stuttered, "Just like your brothers, huh? You think you're too good for Pa's land. You're running off and leaving everything he worked for behind?"

"I ain't got Pa's land. You've got it, and you divvied up between me and Kirk what Pa always said was too poor for planting. Kirk's no better off than me so I'll be handing my house and land over to him."

"You'll do no such thing. I'll take it over," Aiden said, yanking on the lead of the ox. The ox resisted so he wrapped the rope around his wrist good and tight.

"You seem to forget, Aiden, that I insisted on getting a signed deed for each of us. All you wanted to do was give us your word of mouth, and I knew that no truth had ever come out of that mouth. I'm fetching that deed with me when we leave, and I'll send it to Kirk when I'm sure we won't be coming back. And then only when I'm sure he won't cower down to you like he always does. For once, you'll have no control over either of us."

Aiden spurred his horse and swung him back to the path, forgetting he had wrapped the ox lead around his wrist. The horse was startled and broke out into a gallop. The weight of the ox lifted the rider right out of his saddle, and he hit the ground, knocking the breath out of him. The horse took off running leaving a cloud of dust behind him. It was all Rafe could do to keep from laughing when he saw the embarrassment and humiliation on his brother's face. He reached down to give him a hand to help lift him up, but Aiden refused. Rafe stepped back.

"You got a right far piece to walk that old ox home. He's stubborn as a mule, just like you." And with that, Rafe picked up the plow and balanced it across his back, walking rapidly towards his own barn. He hollered out to Dora who was watching the exchange between the two brothers from the safety of the porch.

"Start packing, woman. We've got our answer and we're headin' west!"

CHAPTER TWO
SAYING GOODBYE

O nce Rafe made up his mind, he didn't waste any time. Since he wasn't planting fields or mending fences, he had plenty of time to devote to getting ready for their move. He'd acquired a list from the storekeeper in the town of the type of supplies the men from the wagon trains had bought to prepare for their trip west. He'd put a lot of thought into the process and felt he was ready as he would ever be. The wagon was almost loaded except for the household things and his own personal papers.

"It's your job to do, Rafe. I can't read the words on those papers," she'd told him the night before, and now, the day before they were to leave, he was sitting on the bed going through each piece to see if there were any papers pertaining to Kirk. He would leave him the deed to his land, even though he'd told Aiden he was going to take it with him.

Their mother had given Rafe all her family records before she died knowing that he'd be the one most likely to preserve them. She had also given him a strongbox—a french coffer she had called it—and it held a few family treasures. There was nothing of great value in it except for a few pieces of silver and four gold coins. He began to sort out the papers.

His mother had kept everything, even the papers of her Uncle George Bedinger of the US Senate. He had never married and was one of the early settlers of the Kentucky Wilderness along with Daniel Boone and Frederick Starns, a German immigrant. The first paper he pulled out was a copy of a Revolutionary War Pension Application where George had applied to receive a pension for his service. He read a few lines from it. "In the spring of 1779... we arrived at Fort Boonesborough on 7 April and found Capt. John Holden with only about fifteen men under his command and the fort in great distress and imminent danger in consequence of Mr. Starns and a party of ten or twelve having left the fort a day or two before... Nearly all of them fell into the hands of the Indians. One who made his escape (Joseph, Jr.) got to the fort about two hours after we did and gave information about the defeat of Starns and his party. Fortunately for us, we had missed the path at the time the Indians who killed Capt. Starns and his party were passing on it..."[1]

He quit reading. His own grandfather had told him the story and he cringed thinking of what the Starns men had endured at the hands of the Shawnee raiders. An armed party had gone in search of them and made a gruesome discovery when they arrived. The Indians had mutilated the bodies. One man's heart had been cut out and another's foot was missing.

Rafe shivered. He picked up all the papers and stuffed them in the box without sorting through them. He would just take them all except for the deed. Kirk didn't care about such things anyway. Now his thoughts went to more pressing things. There were savage Indians to the west just like the ones in his grandfather's notes. They'd been lucky to have no Indian raids or skirmishes for years in Kentucky. His parents had experienced them and even Aiden, the oldest, had vague memories of arrows flying through the air from warriors with drawn bows and tomahawks. Thankfully, Rafe had never known that fear. Their home was in a safe place, but here he was moving the two people he loved most to a land of unknowns. Was it too late to back out now? His crops should already be in the ground and he'd sold everything to Kirk.

Dora stuck her head in the door. "Have you seen Tom? Just when I need him, he cuts out." He was still sitting on the bed. He looked up at her as if he hadn't heard her clearly.

His pained expression alarmed her. "Rafe, what's wrong?" she asked.

He patted the bed beside him. "Come sit down, Dora."

She did as he asked and waited.

"Do you remember Colin's letter about the Indians killing his wife's husband?"

"I remember," she said. Then it dawned on her. He was afraid for her and Tom. She reached out and took his hand. "Rafe," she said. "We all made this decision together. I know there are dangers and Tom does too. We've talked about it, remember?"

"I just got so caught up into it, I didn't give enough thought to the risks. We can still back out. Kirk can help me get my crops in the ground and I can slowly pay him back for the farm. I don't think we're too much behind. It's been a cold spring anyway."

She put her finger over his lips. "Shh," she said. "We're going and that's all there is to it. We've come too far to back out now. I'm not afraid."

He felt a huge sense of relief. With a woman like Dora by his side, it would all work out.

~

DORA EYED the contents of the wood crates spread across the kitchen floor. Rafe had hastily made the crates from rough-cut lumber recycled from the milk cow's stall inside the barn. The crates, along with an old trunk that had traveled across the ocean with Dora's seafaring great-grandfather, now held all the household goods to be loaded in the wagon. She had studied on what to take, knowing she'd have to pack light. The trunk held their clothes, blankets and quilts. According to family legend, her great-grandfather, Captain Robert Homes had been an important figure in New England. She wondered how their family ended up poor in the hills of Tennessee.

Not a scrap of material was wasted in the McCade household. When Rafe's shirts wore out, they were made into smaller shirts for Tom or put aside for quilt scraps. Dora hadn't a fancy for fine china. Sure, it was pretty to look at, but not practical for everyday use. The few pieces she had were left in the kitchen cabinet and she packed only her ironstone plates, cups and saucers in amongst the cloth goods to keep them from breaking on the bumpy trail. Pots, pans and utensils filled up one of the crates, and some canned goods filled the other. A butter churn, a crock, a jug and a dishpan stood off to one side. She had even utilized the space in the churn and crocks for storage, including space for their few tattered books and Rafe's family Bible. Books were hard to come by and she was bound and determined to get Rafe and Tom to teach her to read someday.

Satisfied that she had everything they would need, she turned around to see what they were leaving behind. It wasn't much. The kitchen table and two chairs looked lost in the middle of the otherwise empty room. Rafe had loaded the other two kitchen chairs in the wagon after their early supper. She brushed the side of the table with her hand as she walked towards the bedroom.

They'd shared some good times round that table. It had seen good harvest years with food aplenty and lean ones where they just scraped by. But through it all, they'd been thankful for whatever the good Lord provided.

She stepped inside the bedroom. An ornate chest of drawers stood against one wall and a bed with a fancy headboard and footboard leaned against another. The set was a gift from Rafe's Ma and by far the best furniture pieces they owned. The bed was Rafe's own bed he'd slept in as a child and Ma had wanted them to have it when they married. It was the bed where Dora had spent her wedding night with Rafe and become a woman; it was where she'd birthed Tom and hoped for more babies. And it was there that she'd suffered three miscarriages in succession and then the stillbirth of little Alice, with her angelic face and perfect little hands and feet. That had been nearly four years ago, and Dora had been lost in a fog and angry with God for most of the year that followed.

She reached up and fingered the locket around her neck that held a wisp of Alice's baby-fine hair. Fresh tears threatened to wash down her cheeks, but she held them back just as she'd been trying to keep her emotions in check for the last week or so. Her hand wandered down to her breast and then to her abdomen. She knew the early signs of pregnancy all too well. After all, she'd experienced them five times already. And here they were once again. She crossed her arms and wrapped them around herself as an automatic defense against the overwhelming heartbreak that she was afraid would come later. She would keep this to herself. Rafe would only worry about her being with child and this was not the time for a man to worry.

She slowly dropped her hands and glanced around the room again. The bed—it was what she'd miss most of all, but she had to be sensible—it was too much weight for the wagon. Rafe assured her there was plenty of lumber to make beds where they were going. A new beginning, that's what Rafe had called it.

She walked around the partition that separated their room from Tom's. It was a half wall—just enough to give them privacy. His bed was smaller and made from hardwood maple crafted by Rafe's own hands. Soft feather mattresses covered both of their beds. She eyed them longingly and wished they could carry them along.

Their little house was plain but clean. She and Rafe had worked hard to keep it maintained, neat and orderly. She would miss it, but the few tears that once again filled the corners of her eyes quickly dissipated when she thought of what lay ahead. She would not let her emotions spoil their joy of new beginnings. What would be would be.

Back in the kitchen, her eyes drifted to the straw broom leaning in the corner. Would she need it, she wondered? It wouldn't take up much room and would be handy to sweep dust out of the wagon. Grabbing the handle and giving the floor one last brush of the straw, she swept the little bit of dirt out the door and into the yard. Rafe was standing by their farm wagon. He'd done a fine job of converting it into a covered wagon. He too had packed and planned carefully for where each item would be placed. There would be room in the wagon for her to sleep and she'd packed plenty of quilts to sleep on. Tom and Rafe would sleep in a canvas tent, but in a pinch they could all three crowd into the wagon if the weather was bad. The inside of the wagon was a little over seven feet high and fifteen feet long.

Dora stood with the broom in her hand and watched Rafe hang a small shovel from the side. The wagon looked strong and majestic with its white canvas. Rafe and Tom had coated the canvas with linseed oil to further waterproof it. The sturdy wheels had iron rims and were made of hickory wood. The entire wagon had been reinforced with iron in the places that would take the heaviest beatings. Rafe was a planner; he'd thought of everything.

Rafe turned toward the house and saw her standing there. He waved his hand and smiled. Smiling back, she thought he looked happier than she had seen him in years. A new beginning without the family friction would be good for all of them.

"Come take a look," he said, motioning her over. His enthusiasm was contagious, and she wasted no time walking to the wagon.

"Here," he said, lifting her up. "You're light as a feather." She gave him a sideways glance and he laughed. "But tough as an eagle," he countered, knowing she didn't like being thought of as a weakling. and she laughed too.

"I hope you've got a stool handy for me to get in and out of the wagon," she said as she steadied herself. "You'll wear your back out lifting me up and down."

"Don't worry, we'll have the milk stool, but I won't bring it out of the barn until after we milk Daisy in the morning."

She propped the broom in the corner. "I hope we've got room for this."

He lowered her to the ground and grinned. "Yep," he said. "I might have to use it for a pillow." He pulled her to him and kissed her. "We're going to miss sleeping in our soft bed."

"That we are," she said, trying to hold the tears back. "I'm going to miss this old place." She pulled her apron up and dabbed at her cheeks. "Just look at me," she said, shaking her head. "I'm a woman grown but actin' like a big old baby."

He pulled her into an embrace and then held her at arm's length looking into her eyes. "Who was it preaching to me yesterday and saying, 'we're going and that's all there is to it'?" He touched her under the chin. "It won't be easy, Dora, but we'll make out."

She grinned. "Yeah, I reckon it was me, and I know we'll make out, but it's hard leaving some things behind." She looked out in the meadow where a large double headstone stood inside a white picket fence. A smaller one was right beside it.

Rafe followed her gaze and spoke. "I meant to tell you; I've asked Kirk to tend her grave along with Ma's and Pa's."

She nodded and leaned into him.

Tom came out of the house holding a rifle. "I know we've got room for this," he said, and handed it to his father.

"Yes, we do," Rafe said with a grin. "It might just keep you from gettin' et up by a big old bear." Rafe started to put it in the wagon but stopped short. He handed the rifle back to Tom. "Let's put it back in the house until we leave in the morning. That's your granddaddy's old Winchester and Aiden wadn't none too happy when Pa gave it to you. I've noticed him sneaking around watching us load up these last few days and he just might want it bad enough to take it out of the wagon."

Tom frowned. "He'd do that, wouldn't he, Pa? Why's Uncle Aiden so mad all the time?"

"He was born that way," Rafe said with a deadpan expression. "My ma always said the midwife dropped him on his head."

Tom stood there wide-eyed and Dora laughed. "Your Pa's just teasing you. He weren't dropped on his head. He's just mean-tempered, that's all. Your grandma was a God-fearin' woman and raised her boys to be the same, but it just didn't take with Aiden. We won't be worrying about him anymore come tomorrow."

"I won't miss him none," Tom said. He looked down at his feet. "But I'll miss Sarah and Little Aiden. They're not a bit like their Pa."

"No, they take after their Mama," Dora said. "How Molly has put up with that man all these years, I'll never know."

"I wonder if they'll come say goodbye?" Tom asked.

Rafe's look was sullen. "Don't count on it." Tom's smile faded.

Dora put her arm around her son's shoulder. He was still a boy with childlike feelings. Sometimes Rafe tended to forget that. "Don't fret," she said, "I'll take you over tonight. I need to say my goodbyes to Molly."

Tom's mood lightened. "Are you comin' with us, Pa?"

"I'd best not. I've tried to get along with Aiden, Lord knows I have. Greed is a terrible thing, boy. Don't ever let it get hold of you like it did your uncle. I'll go say my goodbyes to Kirk and Sarah. You and your ma can meet me there when you leave Aiden's house. We won't stay long 'cause we'll be needing to get a good night's sleep since we'll be leaving at daybreak."

THE LANTERN LIT up the kitchen and made odd shadows dance across the floor as Dora washed the nice china plates they had used for breakfast. It was the last time they would ever use them, and she held each dish carefully before she dried them and put them back in the cabinet. It seemed odd to be going off and leaving things knowing they'd never come back for them. Kirk and Sarah would be moving in as soon as they left. Sarah's mama would stay in their old house. Maybe now they would have some privacy and start a family.

Kirk had bought Rafe's cattle and horses and he also paid him a modest amount for the house and barn. It had taken most of that money to buy supplies for the trip. Hopefully there was enough of it left to restock along the way. Dora worried what they'd do when they ran out, but Rafe said the Lord would provide. It was a comfort believing He would.

The goodbyes had been hard. Life on the farm with his brothers was all Rafe had ever known, and it was equally hard for Tom to leave his cousins. Dora, on the other hand, wasn't leaving family behind; she'd already done that when she married Rafe. She had put aside her fears and was now anxious to be on their way. Her life was wrapped up in Tom and Rafe, and as long as they were all together, she'd be happy. She put the last dish in the cupboard and her eyes swept over the tidy kitchen. The two remaining chairs were tucked neatly under the table and the threadbare rug was at its normal place by the sink. As an afterthought, she reached down and picked it up. It would fit nicely between the water barrel and the wagon to keep the noise down. She tucked it under her arm and headed for the bedroom. Rafe was taking his sweet time getting ready and she needed to prod him on. Tom had already hitched up the horses to the wagon. Just as she got to the door, she bumped into Rafe on his way out. He was carrying one of the feather mattresses, but it looked about half its normal size.

"Whoa," he said with a faint smile, as they almost collided. "I decided to take our mattress," he said. "Or at least part of it." He held it up. There was a rip on one side and about half the down feathers had been taken out. "I cut it in half. Maybe you can stitch it up as we ride today. You'll need something more comfortable to sleep on than the floor of the wagon."

A tear slipped down her face. She didn't want to look in the room and see what the other half looked like. There were probably feathers all over the floor, but it didn't matter. Rafe was always thinking of her and it touched her heart. She hurriedly wiped her tears away with the back of her hand. "My sewing basket is easy to get at," she said. "I'll make short work of it."

Rafe cupped his hands around her face, and with his rough thumbs brushed away the tears she'd missed. "Don't worry, Dora. We've prayed over this and I feel strong this is what God is leading us to do."

She smiled. "I'm not worried anymore, Rafe. I feel it too—I truly do."

"Are you ready, then?"

"I have one more thing to do before we go."

His hand moved from her face to her shoulders and he gave them a gentle squeeze. "I figured you did. Take your time. Tom has already picked you a handful of flowers. He and I will wait in the wagon."

Holding a bouquet of wildflowers in one hand, Dora opened the gate to the small cemetery with the other and walked inside, not bothering to shut it behind her. The headstones were straight ahead, and she walked to the larger one first. The grave beneath held the remains of Rafe's parents. They had taken her in like their own when she married Rafe. Rafe's ma loved all of her sons, but Dora knew that Rafe was her favorite, probably because of his kind and gentle spirit. It could be why Aiden took such a strong disliking to Rafe, but it had never seemed to bother the other boys. Ma McCade had died first and then Pa not two months behind her of a broken heart. Dora would never forget the love and kindness her mother-in-law bestowed upon her when she lost little Alice.

Rafe's parents were buried side-by-side with only one headstone. The name McCade was engraved along the top of the stone in large letters. Both of Rafe's grandfathers and their brothers had been some of the first settlers in Kentucky following the path of the Wilderness Trail constructed by Daniel Boone in 1775. They'd both fought in the Revolutionary War. They hadn't fought the British themselves, but the Shawnee warriors who had been paid by the British to take scalps from the settlers. They were the Irish McCades on his Pa's side, and the German Bedingers on his Ma's side.

Dora placed two flowers on the graves of her in-laws and traced the lettering on the granite with her fingertip. She knew the words well.

Benjamin Rufas McCade *born* Oct. 17, 1790 *died* Sept 12, 1848

Sarah Bedinger McCade *wife of* Benjamin *born* April 26, 1792 *died* Juy 10, 1848

She moved over to the smaller stone. Ma McCade had ordered it from Philadelphia. It was an arched stone about three feet tall with a relief carving of a lamb at the top. She knelt on her knees to trace the words.

In Memory of Mary Alice
infant daughter of Rafe and Dora McCade
August 20, 1847

Dora picked the remaining flowers out of the bunch one by one and placed them against the stone. As she did so, she breathed in the fresh Kentucky air and began to speak.

"Lord, I ain't quite forgiven you yet for taking my sweet Alice away before I ever got to know 'er. And I reckon you feel the same about me for being mad at you. I'll make a bargain with you: I'll forgive you, and if I've sinned against you by holdin' on tight to this grudge, please forgive me. I don't take much stock in what you said in the old book about babies payin' for the sins of their fathers and mothers. I think Jesus done away with that silliness when you sent him here amongst us.

"Lord, I don't ask you for much, but I'm askin' now for you to give this baby inside me a fightin' chance. I'll do my best to protect her and I expect you to hold up your end of the bargain.

"Lord, I feel bad about leaving little Alice behind, but I don't think she's in that grave nohow. I think she's up there at Jesus's feet playing with all the other little girls who have been took to heaven before and since. Anyways, watch over her and tell her about me so she'll know me when I get there. Amen."

She stood up and put her hand on the gravestone. "Bye Alice. I'm leavin' you in good hands. I love you baby girl." She walked by the other graves and nodded her head. "Bye Ma and Pa. Watch over her, you hear?"

She felt a sweet spirit in the air when she passed Ma's grave and she could almost hear her say, "I will, dear girl. Be at peace."

She walked out and closed the gate behind her. It was the first time she hadn't cried when walking away from Alice's grave. She waved at Tom and Rafe who were watching her. "I'm ready," she said and started running across the field. The sun shone bright on the tall Kentucky bluegrass in the pasture. The spikelets on the seed heads had already formed and they waved in the breeze as if to give them a final farewell.

CHAPTER THREE
ON THE TRAIL

T hey were two weeks out and it had been an uneventful trip so far. The wagon road was dotted with small farms along the way, and they'd been invited to spend one night in a farmer's barn when a sudden storm had hit. Other nights, they'd camped in wooded areas where they felt safer than out in the open.

The weather was excellent on this particular morning when they started out, and they covered nearly twenty miles before they came to a good stopping place. Rafe was unhitching the horses from the wagon while Dora was warming up the leftover stew from the night before. Biscuits were baking in the black dutch oven resting on the coals. Twigs and firewood were plentiful at the edge of the woods and Tom had gathered what they needed. The campfire was burning brightly, and Rafe was pleased with the spot they'd chosen to spend the night. A bubbling springhead fed the small stream running down the hillside where it would eventually empty out into the Wabash River. The spring would provide good clean water for refilling their barrels when they left the site.

Their team of horses had no trouble pulling the wagon and its contents thus far and were not likely to since Dora packed lighter than most. She had scoffed at a family they'd met two days back who were carrying a piano in the back of their wagon. "They'll be throwing that thing out somewhere along the trail," she said. "It's not worth killing the horses over."

Rafe had agreed and was pondering over it as he tethered the horses where there was a good stand of grass. They'd made good time with a light load, good weather and good wagon trails to follow. They'd been eight days on the trail when they'd stopped overnight at Fort Boonesborough. That had been five days back. The information they gathered at the fort had buoyed their spirits. If they kept their momentum and conditions were favorable, Rafe figured they'd be in St. Louis in fifteen days, maybe less.

When the ropes were tied securely, he started back to the fire, but stopped suddenly. There was a noise in the distance. As it came closer, he could hear the sound of a wagon creaking and a heavy plodding of hooves on the trail they'd just come up. Someone was traveling when they should have been making camp.

"Hal-loo," a voice boomed in the night. "We're comin' in. Mind if we share your campfire?"

Rafe nodded his head at Tom. Tom understood and ran to the back of the wagon to get the shotgun, staying just out of sight.

"Come on in." Rafe shouted. "We've got a good fire going."

The wagon came into sight with four large oxen pulling it. There was a milk cow and a sorrel horse being led by a rope tied to the back of the wagon. Rafe's own milk cow was already grazing alongside the horses. He relaxed when the wagon pulled to a stop and the driver stepped down. It was a man a few years younger than himself but a whole lot bulkier. The man reached back to steady the arm of a young woman who was stepping down from the wagon. A small child jumped down behind her and as they came closer, he could see it was a young boy.

"You're late making camp," Rafe said, "but I can't say much. We've not been here more'n an hour ourselves."

"It is late. We started to stop back on the trail, but I wanted to get in as much daylight as I could. Then we smelled your smoke and figured it would be nice to have some company."

"Come on to the fire. We're eatin' leftovers, but you're welcome to share what we have. I'm Rafe and this here's my wife, Dora. That's my son, Tom, back by the wagon." He gestured to Tom. "Come on out, boy."

The man held out his hand and Rafe shook it. "I'm Clay Campbell." He turned to the woman and put his arm around her. "This is Ellie, my wife, and our son, Jimmy." He tipped his hat to Dora. "Nice to meet you, ma'am."

Dora smiled. "Y'all welcome to share our vittles. Ain't much, but it'll keep your stomachs from grumblin'."

"Don't mind if we do. I killed and dressed two rabbits this afternoon. We can add those to the spit." Clay walked to the side of the wagon and lifted the two rabbits out of a wooden pail. "They're clean and ready to put on the fire."

Rafe helped Clay tend to the oxen and Ellie walked over to the stream to stake out the milk cow near the McCade's cow and their horses. After they finished eating, the women cleaned up from the meal while Rafe and Clay talked about the trail and what lay ahead. The Campbells were only going as far as St. Louis. Clay's brother was the captain of a steamship and wanted Clay to come out and work for him. It would be a better life than sharecropping like they'd been doing. Tom taught young Jimmy how to play Jacks until the small rubber ball rolled out of sight and Jimmy started crying when they couldn't find it.

Ellie walked over and picked him up. "It's time for this one to be settled in bed," she said. She looked at Dora and smiled. "About time for his Ma too. It's been a long day's ride. Thank you for sharing your supper with us."

"Didn't mind at all," she said. "We were glad to share your rabbits too. We'll be turnin' in shortly ourselves. Y'all have a good night's sleep."

When Rafe turned out the next morning, he saw that Ellie had brought the cow in closer and was milking it. She was an early riser and had already added kindling and a log to what was left of last night's fire. She looked up when she heard him stoking the fire and adding another log. "I'm not usually up before Clay, but Jimmy woke up hungry for milk. That boy, he's always hungry."

"All boys are. Tom can eat me under the table any day of the week." The fire was catching up and Rafe added some dry sticks. "I see you moved your cow up close."

"Yes, Bessie pulled her stake up sometime during the night and was grazing in the woods on the other side of the creek. When I picked up her lead, I noticed she had the tremors—I guess from walking in the water. I know it sounds crazy, but I moved her near to the fire to get her warmed up."

Rafe looked concerned. "That's strange. The creek's not that cold this time of year."

"That's what I thought but look—she's shaking again."

He watched and sure enough, it looked like the cow was having a cold chill. Something was niggling in the back of his mind. What was it? He heard Dora as she jumped lightly from the tailgate of the wagon. Tom wasn't far behind and walked to the fire and rubbed his hands over it to warm himself. Rafe ruffled his sleep-tousled hair.

"It's time to get old Daisy milked, boy. Mrs. Campbell has already got a half-gallon in her pail." Tom wiped the sleep from his eyes and walked to the side of the wagon, lifting a tin bucket from a peg.

Dora was getting the pans out to fry some bacon. "Howdy," she said with a grin. "You're up and making us look lazy this morning."

"Jimmy was begging for milk," she said. "He finally quieted down. Maybe he went back to sleep." About that time, a loud cry came from the back of the wagon.

"Mama, I'm hungry."

"See," she said. "When he's hungry, he's like a big old bear. He takes after his daddy." She stopped milking the cow and called out to her husband. "Clay, go ahead and bring the boy out to the fire. Bessie's not giving as much milk as usual, but I've got enough that he'll be happy." Clay stepped out of the wagon carrying Jimmy in his arms.

"You baby him too much," Clay said as Ellie started straining the milk.

"Me? Look at you holding that big boy in your arms like he can't walk."

Clay laughed and put him down. It didn't take Jimmy long to notice Tom walking downhill with the milk pail and he raced to catch up with him.

"Can I help? Please. I know how to milk a cow."

Ellie called him back. "Don't be tellin' tall tales," she said. "You've never milked a cow. Get back here right now."

He came back but he wasn't happy about it. "I wanna go, Mama. I'm not hungry anymore."

"Listen to me, Jimmy. I had to round up Bessie from the creek bank, then bring her here to get warm by the fire because the poor thing was shivering so! You've been crying for milk, so now you're gonna sit here and drink it."

Tom looked at the cow as he walked past her to milk his own cow. "She sure looks cold to me. She's shakin' all over."

Dora's head turned when she heard Tom's comment. "Wait, let me take a look," she said, hurrying over. She ran her fingers along the side of the cow's ribs and watched as she continued to tremor. Ellie had finished straining the milk and began pouring it into a tin cup.

"Lord, have mercy", Dora said. She ran back and knocked the cup out of Ellie's hand. It hit the ground and made a loud sound when it bounced against a rock. Milk splashed on the wagon wheel.

"Don't let that boy have any of that milk," she shouted in a fiery command. Everyone stood back in shock.

"What is it Dora?" Rafe asked, looking at his wife with concern. The others were too taken aback to speak, and Jimmy started crying.

"It's the cow, Rafe. See those tremors? I'll wager she's been grazing on snake-root and if she has, the milk will poison the boy. I've seen it kill a grown man."

Ellie looked horrified and pulled Jimmy into her lap.

"Where was the cow tied last night?" Dora asked.

Ellie stammered as she spoke. "I-I found her wandering in the woods across the creek."

"Show me where," Dora said. They all walked behind Ellie as she led them across a fallen log to the spot where she'd found Bessie. Dora searched the ground, pulling the leaves back with her hands and continued for a few yards.

"There it is! This is where she's been nibbling on it." She pointed to a small green plant covered in tiny white blooms. It was easy to see that the top of the plant had been clipped off as if it had been cut by shears. "It grows by crick banks and cows are greedy over it. My pa would find the plants and pull 'em out by the roots fearing our milk cows would get ahold of 'em. Tremblin' is the first sign that a cow's been poisoned by snake root. Thank the good Lord above that your baby didn't drink the milk. He'd be gone before the day is up."

Ellie turned pale and fainted right down to the ground. Dora stooped down and patted her on the face. "Ellie, honey," she said, shaking her slightly. Her eyes opened. "You didn't drink any of it, did you?" Ellie shook her head, no.

Rafe helped Ellie to her feet while Clay picked Jimmy up and stood there too stunned to speak for a moment. He finally found his voice.

"Mrs. McCade, I don't know how to thank you. Our whole family might have died right here on the trail if you hadn't stopped us."

"Ya' don't owe me any thanks; it's the good Lord who made me know what it was. We had a neighbor that died of the sickness back home. They knew it was the sickness 'cause the cow was trembling, just like your Bessie."

"Will Bessie die?" Clay asked with a worried look.

Dora was wringing her hands. She knew how much she and Rafe were dependent on their own cow's milk and she hated to be the bearer of bad news. "I reckon it depends on how much she ate. But if it was my cow, I'd put her down because somewhere between here and St. Louis, she's more'n likely gonna die anyway. If you do put her down, you and Rafe need to bury her deep where nothin' can get ahold of her 'cause her meat is just as poison as her milk."

Ellie looked pleadingly at her husband. "Can't we just wait and see what happens, Clay?"

He turned to Dora. "What if she doesn't die? How long does the poison stay in her system?"

"That I don't know. I guess you could wait and see if she gets over it, but I don't know how long you'd have to wait until the milk is safe to drink again." She gave Rafe a questioning look. His slight shrug indicated the decision was up to her. Between biscuit making and the amount each of them had been drinking, it had been taking every ounce of milk their cow produced. Without thinking, she rubbed her hand against her tummy. She would need to drink milk to stay healthy for her baby. Was it growing inside her or would it shed from her body as three others had done before it?

Ellie was growing increasingly anxious. "What'll we do, Clay? Is there somewhere else we could buy a cow?"

Clay patted her hand and tried to appease her. "We'll stop at some farms along the way and see. Don't worry."

Dora had her doubts. If the farms ahead were like the ones they had passed, they didn't stand a chance of finding a cow. Most families had one milk cow and would never think of selling it. She looked from one to the other and made up her mind. Her family could cut back a mite and share Daisy's milk with Jimmy and if both families cooked together, they'd get by.

Before she changed her mind, she spoke up. "If you want to ride the trail with us, we'll see fit to share with you. Daisy's been giving a good bit of milk lately."

Clay looked at the woman in front of them and knew not everyone would be that generous. He tipped his hat. "That's awful kind of you," he said.

Ellie was crying. She blamed herself for not checking to be sure Bessie was staked securely. She and Clay could do without milk, but Jimmy needed it to stay healthy. She was touched by the generous offer from this family they barely knew. They had a growing lad too.

Bessie had been with them since she and Clay had married. She loved this cow with the big eyes, but it was obvious just looking at Bessie that she was suffering.

Clay's voice broke through her thoughts. "Ellie, I don't want to take any chances with Bessie. Let's get it over with and bury her here. Let's face it; she's not going to get any better."

Ellie nodded. "Just lead her off somewhere so I don't have to see it done," she answered.

The men led the cow away while Dora tried to comfort Ellie. "It'll be alright," she said, putting her arm around the other woman's shoulder. "It's not far to St. Louis and you can get you another cow. Meanwhile, we've got plenty to share."

Tom finished milking Daisy and brought the bucket to Dora. "Look, Ma. I've never seen Daisy give so much milk at one time! It's like she knew she had more mouths to feed."

Dora smiled softly. "It wadn't up to Daisy, son. God knew what was needed and He provided."

Tom poured some milk into his own tin cup and handed it to Jimmy who eagerly took it and drank every drop. Ellie smiled through her tears as she watched it drip down his chin. Dora offered up another prayer and knew everything was going to be okay. She was glad to have the company of another woman. It would be good for the men too. Rafe had inquired about joining a wagon train so they wouldn't have to travel alone, but they had waited too late. Now it was on to St. Louis where they would take leave of the Campbells, replenish their supplies and move on to pick up the Santa Fe Trail as planned.

CHAPTER FOUR
ST. LOUIS

Rafe sat on his horse overlooking the massive body of water before him. His brother had written about the Mississippi River but Rafe had laughed when reading it to Dora. "That brother of mine tends to stretch the truth a mite when he gets excited," he'd told her. "I've never seen a river anywhere near that wide." But here it was, and every bit as wide as Colin had said, and maybe even wider since it had rained for two solid days and nights and the banks were overflowing. They had run across another family on the trail who told them the river was bad to flood so he had left the others back at camp this morning and rode ahead to see if the trail was passable. It was, but barely.

If they had been traveling alone, he would have stayed put at the camp for another day, but the Campbell family was still with them, and with Clay's help, Rafe was sure they could get through the wet spots with a little push and shove on the wagons if needed. By mid-afternoon they should reach St. Louis which was about two miles due North of the spot where he was now seated on his horse.

He was tempted to go further up the trail, but he remembered what his brother had told him about river pirates. It would be safer to have Clay along if they ran into trouble. He had proven himself to be a good man. His huge shoulders and arms wielding an ax could bust up firewood in no time. He was good with a gun and had shown Rafe a new contraption he had never seen before. It was a cylinder-shaped copper wire mesh sleeve loaded with pellets. Rafe had watched as Clay poured the powder charge into the gun's bore, dropped the wire cylinder into the muzzle over the charge, and with the ramrod, rammed the entire load in place.[1] It was fast and easy and when they'd gone out hunting the day before, Clay dropped a buck from a far greater distance than Rafe had thought possible.

Rafe would be sorry to leave the Campbell family in St. Louis. They would be good to ride the trail with all the way to Colorado, but Clay had promised to help his brother in his steamboat business. The great fire of St. Louis had destroyed much of the town and a good many of the steamboats. His brother's boat was one of the few to survive. And Rafe could understand how it was to want to settle down with family around. He'd made the same kind of promise to Colin and he was bound and determined to keep it. He gave the river one more sweep of his eyes and abruptly turned his horse around, eager to head back to camp.

The abrupt turn saved his life; he was sure of it. As soon as he turned, he heard the sound of a bullet whiz through the air right where his head had been one second before. He looked around but didn't see anyone. Anger replaced the eagerness he'd felt before. Some careless hunter, he thought. Granted, the place was remote, but he would never shoot at something unless he could see it clearly. It would be nice if others would do the same.

∽

CLAY HAD the teams hitched by the time he made it back to camp and by mid-afternoon and after a rough go of it, both wagons were now stopped on the eastern bank of the Mississippi where he'd been before. The trail had been easy enough to navigate for one man by horse, but when retracing his steps with two wagons, it was a different story. He and Clay took turns pushing and shoving and digging wheels out along the muddy trail while Tom took lead of their horses and Dora took the lead of the Campbells' oxen. The oxen were better suited for the conditions but Rafe's horses were a tough breed and held their own. Everyone was tired and dirty but thankful that the rain had stopped, and the sun was shining brightly on the wide expanse of water in front of them.

"I could use a bit of a rest and a bite to eat before we head into the city," Clay said as he got down from the wagon and joined Rafe.

Rafe looked at his new friend and laughed. "And if I look anything like you, we could both use a bath. How about a good dunkin' in the Mississippi?"

Clay clapped him on the back. "Don't mind if I do," he said. "I'll race you."

Rafe put one foot in front of the other, but Dora grabbed hold of his suspenders. "Wait up," she said. He lost his momentum and almost knocked both of them backwards.

"What in tarnation?" he asked.

"If you're going to take a proper bath, you need to take a bar of soap and some clean clothes with you." She turned loose of his suspenders. "I'll get 'em from the back of the wagon."

Clay was standing there looking on in amusement. "Looks like I'll beat you there after all," he said.

"Not so fast, Clay Campbell." It was Ellie's voice. He turned around and she was standing at the back of their wagon. "You'll be takin' a proper bath too. I'll get your clothes."

"I ain't never heard of a proper bath before, woman. Let me go about my business," he said.

"Well now you have," she said, following Dora's lead. "And a proper bath you'll be havin'." She lifted Jimmy out of the back of the wagon along with a small round basket. And take the boy with you. He could stand a good scrubbing."

Dora grinned and handed Rafe a bundle wrapped in a flour sack. "Here you go," she said. "I'd send Tom with you, but at the mention of a bath, he disappears."

Both men took the clothes their women gave them and headed toward the river, this time without as much enthusiasm. Clay hung his head sheepishly and then spoke. "As much as I've enjoyed your company, Rafe McCade, I'll be somewhat glad to take leave of you once we get to St. Louis."

Rafe looked at him in surprise. "And why is that?"

Clay grinned. "Cause if Ellie was to stay around your woman much longer, I'd be in trouble, my friend."

While the men bathed, Dora and Ellie chatted as they prepared a hurried meal of bacon and biscuits leftover from breakfast. Theirs was a free and easy companionship after more than a week of sharing meal preparations. They had also shared matters of the heart and found much comfort in each other's company.

Ellie confided that she and Clay wanted more children and she was distressed that it hadn't happened yet. Dora told Ellie of the three miscarriages, but she wasn't comfortable sharing about losing Alice. With her heightened hormones at play, it required too much emotional energy to speak of it. And it wouldn't be fair to tell Ellie about her pregnancy when she hadn't even told Rafe.

Tom watched Rafe, Clay and Jimmy play in the water from his hiding place beyond the treeline where he had slipped when talks of a bath began. They looked to be having so much fun, he wished he hadn't hidden at all. He started out to the clearing but stopped short when he saw two men on foot headed through the pines leading up to the riverbank where the others were bathing. Something didn't feel right about the way they were zig-zagging back and forth as though they didn't want to be seen. It frightened him but he had the presence of mind to run quietly to the back of the wagon and pull the old Winchester out. He grabbed his Ma's arm and pointed in the direction of the men.

"Here, let me have the gun," she whispered when she saw the men. "Run back to the wagon and fetch your daddy's shotgun. They're not paying us any mind yet, but they're sure up to no good."

Tom jumped in the wagon and pulled out Rafe's gun. His mama whispered again and pointed to the right. "You head down to the bank on the right-hand side and I'll go this way. Don't get too close though. They're dangerous men."

Tom was frightened, but his mother's calm voice steadied him. "I'll get their attention," she said. "If they pull a gun or a knife, you make yourself known behind 'em. Shoot for their legs if you think they're aiming to harm either one of us."

She turned to Ellie. "You might want to get Clay's shotgun."

"I don't know how to use it," she said, wringing her hands.

"Has he got another gun?"

Ellie's eyes were wide with fear, but she nodded. "He's got a pistol."

"Get it then," Dora whispered. "It's simple enough. Your little boy's down there. If something happens to me, you just point the gun, cock the hammer and go to blastin', you hear?" Ellie nodded again and made her way quickly to their wagon.

There was a large boulder between the wagon and the men, and Dora kept out of sight as she made her way toward the bank. Meanwhile Tom started off in the direction she had pointed so he would be behind the men. "Make sure you stay out of my line of fire," she whispered. He nodded and moved swiftly.

The men were focused on the bathers. They hadn't seen Tom and had sized up the women as no threat to them at all. But they'd never met a woman like Dora. They were closing in on the bank when she appeared out of the blue and yelled.

"Hey, you two! Raise your hands over your heads." She said it loud enough for Rafe and Clay to hear and they looked toward the bank in surprise. The two men stopped cold and looked back at Dora. She made a formidable sight standing there with a gun pointed straight toward them, but one of them made a move to take something out of his waistband.

Tom yelled from behind them. "She said to raise your hands over your heads," he said boldly. "And she told me to shoot you if you made any other moves." The men hesitated.

Rafe and Clay were quickly making their way out of the water, Clay much more modestly than Rafe. "I'd listen to her if I was you," Rafe said. "She's my woman and she's a better shot than both of you put together. And that's my boy back there with the other gun. He can shoot a fly off a deer's back."

He was back on the bank and pulling on his pants. "You boys have picked on the wrong woman. She'd as soon shoot you and be done with you. I'm surprised she gave you any kind of warning."

They both raised their hands. A knife gleamed brightly in the sunlight.

"Drop that knife and kick it away from you," Dora hollered. He dropped it to the ground and sent it flying down the hill with his foot.

Clay was holding back in the water with Jimmy. He was embarrassed to have Dora see him unclothed.

"I ain't lookin' at you, Clay Campbell," she said. "I got my eyes on these two river rats. Get out of there quick and get dressed."

Clay scrambled up the bank and hurriedly dressed himself. "Run on up the hill to your ma," he said to Jimmy, swatting him on the backside. The boy didn't hesitate and took off running naked as a jaybird.

The two men were standing still, both with arms raised. Clay and Rafe moved simultaneously and got behind them. "Lower your arms slowly and put them behind your backs." One did as he was told and Rafe grabbed his hands and swiftly tied them up with his belt. When Clay went to do the same, the other man kicked back with his foot and knocked Clay off balance. It sent Clay sprawling down the bank. The man pulled a knife out of his waistband and went diving after him. It was obvious that he intended to kill Clay and try to escape by jumping in the water, and it happened so fast, no one had time to react.

Rafe turned around when Dora shouted out. Tom had gone closer when he thought they were out of danger. "Here Pa," he said, and tossed the shotgun to Rafe. He caught it up but there wasn't much he could do while the men were fighting over the knife. If he shot now while they were on top of each other, he would probably kill both of them. Rafe started toward them, looking for a way to get them separated, but they were tumbling down the bank together fighting over control of the knife. Clay was stronger but the other man had more fighting experience and it was just a matter of seconds before Clay cried out as the knife blade sunk in. The man pulled the knife out and raised his arm up high to give one final stab. Finally, it gave Rafe the target he needed to shoot and Rafe aimed for the lifted shoulder and hit his mark The force of the blast caused a forward momentum and the man tumbled down the rocky bank and hit the water. Rafe walked to the edge and looked down. It wasn't a pretty sight when lifeless eyes stared up at him.

Rafe was shaken but he ran to Clay's side. Ellie was already there, and she was crying. She looked pleadingly into Rafe's eyes. "Is he alive?" she asked between sobs.

He looked down at his friend whose eyes were closed. The crimson on his fresh clean shirt was spreading wider. Rafe panicked and turned around. "Dora!" he called. "Quick, bring your medicine bag!"

She touched him on the shoulder. "I'm already here," she said, trying to remain calm for Ellie's sake. "Move back so I can get to him."

Dora placed a finger along Clay's neck and felt for a pulse, then breathed a sigh of relief. "He's alive!"

CHAPTER FIVE

Dora cleaned and dressed the wound on Clay's right side and with Ellie's help, she wrapped a strip from a sheet around his upper body hoping the pressure would help stop the bleeding.

"You lost some blood," she said to their friend who was now laying on a quilt staring up at her, but it ain't nearly as bad as it first looked. You can thank the good Lord above that it didn't hit any of your vital parts. It's just a flesh wound, and it'll heal. The knife blade went right between two of your ribs." She picked up the knife from where it had dropped to the ground. "The blade being so sharp didn't do as much damage as a duller blade would."

Rafe and Ellie had stood close by while Dora was working on Clay. Tom had stood back with Jimmy to keep him from seeing his Pa bleeding, but now they had come closer and Tom was curious. "Can I see the knife, Ma?" he asked.

Dora looked up at Rafe and he nodded. She wiped the blade clean on one of the rags she'd used to clean the wound and handed it to Tom. "Be careful; it's sharp," she said.

Tom took it and looked it over. "It's an Arkansas toothpick," he said. "I've heard of 'em but never seen one."

"It'll make a good souvenir for Clay," Rafe said. "It'll remind him of why he's got that scar on his chest."

"Let the boy keep the knife," Clay said. "I won't need no reminder. I've seen too much of that blade already."

Rafe looked at the knife, then at Tom. "If you want it, you can keep it," he said. "You've seen what it can do to a man, so be careful with it." He looked down the bank and then back at Tom again. "And now you've seen what a gun can do to a man. I've killed animals before and not thought much of it because it's food for the table, but killing this man is somethin' I'll have to live with the rest of my life. I snuffed the light out of somebody's soul."

"But he didn't have much of a soul, Pa," Tom argued. "He woulda killed Clay if you hadn't killed him."

"I know that, son, and it had to be done. But still, he was a man and I hated doin' it."

"Let it be, Rafe," Dora said. "I know it pains you, but one more stab from that knife and Clay would be covered up with this quilt instead of laying on top of it. Let's try to get 'im in the wagon." She examined Clay's bandage to be sure it hadn't started bleeding again. When she was satisfied it hadn't, she spoke to him.

"Clay, can you stand up if Tom and Rafe give you a hand?" she asked. "You're too stout for any of us to carry."

"I think so," he said.

"Be easy," she said as they got on each side of him. "Hold him under his arms and lift until he's on his feet. Then keep him steady until he can stand on his own."

He made it to his feet and with their help he walked slowly up the bank and to the back of his wagon. Dora, Ellie and Jimmy followed behind carrying everything else. The prisoner stayed seated on the ground, still in shock at seeing his partner killed.

"We'll take you both into St. Louis," Rafe said when he got Clay settled and walked back down to the bank. "I'm going to untie you long enough for you to help me load your friend's body on the back of my wagon, but if you've got any notions about tryin' to get away, you better think it over careful-like. That woman up there is a better shot than I am."

He untied him and between the two of them, they carried the body to a tree near the wagon. "What was his name?" Rafe asked.

The man spat on the ground. "What does it matter to you?"

"It matters," Rafe said. "If I have to remember killing a man, I want to know his name. I'll try to find his family and break it to 'em."

"Luther Barr," the man finally said. "He ain't got no family."

"Are you the man who shot at me this morning when I was on my horse?"

"That was Luther. I don't have a gun."

"Was he a friend to you?" Rafe asked.

"No, I ain't knowed him for long. He was a mean one—probably needed killin'."

"Probably," Rafe said. "I just wish it wadn't me that had to do it."

Rafe tied the man up again—this time, both his hands and his feet, and he leaned him against another tree. They talked for a minute and Rafe walked back to the wagon.

Dora looked at the food she and Ellie had spread out for lunch and thought about the easy camaraderie they had shared while preparing it. They had talked of pleasant things and were blissfully unaware of the danger they were about to face. They had all been hungry after a morning of struggling to get the wagons through the mud-caked trail. Now she had no appetite at all and wondered about the others.

"There's plenty of food," she said to no one in particular, and the only two who paid her any heed were Tom and Jimmy who came running. She motioned to Tom. "Get your cup and Jimmy's and pour you some water from the barrel."

Tom eyed the food hungrily. "Aw, Ma, let him fix his own," he whined.

All it took was a sharp eye from Dora and Tom was scrambling for both cups. While he drew water from the tap on the barrel, Dora brushed an ant off the biscuit she handed to Jimmy. The boy looked up at her with wide eyes and she smiled. "Don't worry," she said, "the ant only took a tiny bite." Jimmy found her words funny and laughed loudly. She laughed too knowing that the laughter was good. It would help release the stress, especially for the boy, from seeing his pa wounded so.

Rafe walked up while they were eating. "Tom, when you and Jimmy finish, you can help me gather some wood for a fire. A cup of coffee would taste awful good right now."

"So we're not going on into St. Louis today?" Dora asked.

"I think we'd best let Clay heal up a mite. The trail ahead has ruts from the rain, and it wouldn't do for 'im to get too shook up."

"What are we going to do with them," she asked, pointing to the men.

"I think we'd best bury the one. His friend says he doesn't have a family, so there'd be no one to claim his body. He told me the man's got a little lean-to up in the woods, so we'll bury him where he lived and carve his name on a stone."

"I'm sorry, Rafe. I know it hurts you havin' done what you had to do, but there's no telling how many lives you saved by doing it."

He didn't say anything, but he nodded. The boys were finished eating. "Come on boys, let's get some firewood." The boys headed towards the woods.

"Keep a watch out," Dora shouted behind them. "There might be more of their kind around."

"I doubt it," Rafe said. "When I talked to the other thief back there, he said they're the only two that work this area. There's a standing agreement among their kind to stay off each other's territory so it'll be okay for a few days until some of the others get wind of what happened and move in."

Dora was sitting on the log that the boys had just vacated. "You know, don't you, that if it hadn't been for Tom's sharp eye, that knife and the other would have been between your shoulder blades and Clay's? Me and Ellie didn't even see what was happening. Oh Lord, both of you might have been dead by now!" She leaned over with her head in her hands.

Rafe sat down beside her. "I guess we should be thankful Tom's not keen on bathing," he said, trying to smile.

Dora looked up at him with tears in her eyes. "I don't know what I'd do if somethin' happened to you, Rafe. I saw poor Ellie's eyes when she thought Clay was dead and I could feel my own heart break for her. It would of broke in a hundred pieces if it had been you lying there."

"You'd make it, Dora. You're a stronger woman than most and you've got a level head on your shoulders. If somethin' happens to me on this trip, I want you and the boy to keep going. Colin will take care of you."

She wrapped her arms around her tummy. "Let's just don't talk about it anymore," she said. "Scoot on out and help those boys gather firewood and we'll get some coffee brewin'. Every one of us is in need of a cup."

Ellie came back out when Rafe was gone.

"How's Clay feeling?" Dora asked.

"He's not in too much pain," she said. "Those herbs you put on 'im must have helped."

"There's a plant for just about everything that ails you," Dora said. "You just have to know the combinations."

"Come to think of it," Ellie said, smiling, "it might not be the plants at all, but the Kentucky moonshine we gave him while you were dressing his wound."

"More than likely," Dora said, smiling back. "Do you want something to eat?" she asked.

"You know, I was hungry before, but I think I'd be sick if I tried to eat something now," she said.

"I know what you mean. I couldn't eat a bite."

"I'm so thankful you and Rafe were with us," Ellie said, wrapping her arms around Dora. "I would have fainted dead away if I was by myself when it happened. You were so brave."

Dora sighed. "I might have looked brave, but I was scared," she said. "Right now I'm as weak as a kitten." She stood up to get a cup of coffee.

"Wait, sit back down. I'll get your coffee." As Ellie filled the cup and handed it to Dora, she smiled. "Clay would say that you need a drink of that Kentucky moonshine. It's good for what ails you."

Dora straightened up. "Oh no, I've got to keep my wits about me," she said, trying to make light of it. The two women looked at each other with mutual respect. They knew the outcome of their afternoon could have been very different indeed.

CHAPTER SIX
ST. LOUIS

A floating palace was the only way Dora knew how to describe the steamboat they had just passed on their ferry ride crossing the river. She had seen pictures of castles and palaces with their heavy brocade curtains and fancy chandeliers in one of Ma McCade's books about the old country, and they weren't nearly as beautiful as this. The smokestacks were decorated with cutouts of exotic feathers and ferns. Colorful pennants on the wheelhouse snapped in the breeze. She saw men in fancy suits lounging on the deck playing cards while the ladies carrying parasols chatted by the railings. Dora and Ellie waved when they went by, but no one was paying attention to the ferry and she couldn't blame them because they had all they could feast their eyes upon right there on that big boat. Loud music was blaring across the water from an instrument that she couldn't identify. It seemed it was coming from the pipes atop the cabin of the steamboat where little bursts of steam popped up as the music played.

"It's called a calliope," Clay explained as he and Rafe leaned against the rail beside them. Staying put for the night had done Clay a world of good and he was walking without any assistance.

"It's playing the Virginia Reel. Edward told me all about these boats in his letters. It's the way the folks with lots of money entertain themselves."

"Does your brother have a boat like that?" Dora asked.

"Oh no, his boat carries cargo down the Mississippi. It was one of the few boats of its type that didn't burn in the fire along the waterfront two years ago. The fire destroyed a big part of the town—Edward said over 400 buildings were burned. They still haven't built it all back."

Rafe heard a commotion at the front of the boat and turned to look. He watched as the captain of the ferry jerked their prisoner to a standing position. They had untied his feet to get him on board.

"You sorry rat," the captain yelled. "You think you can escape by slipping in the water, do ye? You're not going to get off that easy. If you try that again, I'll tie you to a paddle, throw you overboard and drag you into shore. I want to see you hang for all the thieving and murdering you've been doing along these riverbanks."

The captain had been happy to hold the man when they boarded the ship. He himself had been a victim and told Rafe there was reward money to be paid for this man and for Luther Barr, the man Rafe had shot. When Rafe told him the reward money would go to his wife and son who had been the ones to hold their guns on the men in the first place, he looked at Dora in amazement. "Lots of men have tried to catch these men, ma'am. My hat's off to you," he said and promptly took his hat off with a flourish. "I'll personally deliver this rat to the sheriff's office and you can pick up your money later." Rafe thanked him as Dora blushed.

As they got closer to the waterfront, Dora could see that the city of St. Louis was huge. Different styles and sizes of steamboats lined the riverfront and more were coming and going up and down the river. Plumes of steam filled the air. She had never seen such a sight. She thought it must be the biggest city in the world. But as they neared the docks, she could see the devastation caused by the fire. Burned out facades of tall buildings stood out starkly against the blue of the sky. Fallen bricks and rubble still lined the waterfront in places.

One of the town leaders was on the ferry and Clay asked him if he knew where his brother's boat was docked. The man pointed, "He's got a booming business, your brother has, Mr. Campbell. Since his boat was one of the few left undamaged after the fire, his cargo services have been in big demand. He's made quite a bit of money and recently bought an even bigger vessel that was built by none other than James Eads, the finest builder of boats since Robert Fulton in the last century. Your brother has come a long way since he began his business, starting off with a flatboat hauling cargo downstream in some of the most dangerous of conditions. But I'm sure you know all that since he's your own brother?"

Dora watched as the men were talking. She could see that Clay was surprised but pleased at the man's compliments about Edward. He shook his head. "No," he said. "My brother is a humble man and not inclined to boast about his business. I came because he said he needed me to work with him and that's what I plan to do."

The ferry had stopped and put down its planks for docking on the beach. Clay tipped his hat to the man he'd been talking to. "Thank you for the information, sir. Maybe I'll be seeing you around town."

"I'm pleased to make your acquaintance, Mr. Campbell." He reached out his hand to shake Clay's. "I'm John O'Fallon, president of the U.S. Bank here in St. Louis, and if you ever need anything, look me up."

"Yes sir, I will. Good day to you."

Mr. O'Fallon tipped his hat to the McCades and joined the line of people leaving the boat.

"He was a nice fella," Dora said when he left them.

"And a handy one to know in case you ever need a loan," Rafe added. "He spoke highly of your brother."

Clay watched as the banker walked down the narrow ramp. "Much more highly than my brother speaks of himself. I would never have known from his letters that he was successful if he hadn't sent money to us from time to time."

Ellie reached for Jimmy and picked him up in her arms. "Let me down, Ma," the boy complained.

"This is no place to get lost, son," Clay said. "You're so fast, your mama can't keep up with you."

"I'll hold on to him," Tom volunteered.

Ellie put the boy down. "Thank you, Tom. Hold on tight. He'll try to scamper away."

Clay motioned to Rafe. "Let's get our wagons unloaded. Ellie can handle ours. I'd better sit this one out. It won't be long before the ferry starts taking on passengers for the trip back across the river."

~

EDWARD SENT a message home to Mary as soon as the McCades and his brother's family arrived at his dock. "Six more for dinner," he wrote. "Clay's here with friends."

Edward's home was ten blocks from the waterfront. It had three bedrooms and was modest compared to the homes near the waterfront. Their first home had been a small cabin with a dirt floor a few miles out of town. When Edward saved enough to buy the steamboat, they decided to move closer where he could keep an eye on his boat. They bought the house from a young family who left for California in search of gold. Edward's gold was right here hauling freight up and down the Mississippi.

Edward Campbell sat at the head of the table and his wife, Mary, sat on his right-hand side. Rafe wasn't paying much attention to the seating arrangements; he was looking at the abundance of food spread out in front of them. Tom, Jimmy, and Edward's three boys were eating in the kitchen while the adults were in the dining room.

They had received a warm welcome from Clay's family and in addition to inviting them to dinner, Edward pressed them to stay in their home.

Dora didn't waste any time accepting. She had not complained about their journey but Rafe knew she was happy to have a nice, clean bed to sleep in again. When they arrived, the first thing she did was ask Mary if she had a wash pan so she could bathe. She was filled with joy when her hostess showed her the bathing room with a large clawfoot tub. Mary ordered the housemaid to warm some water and fill the tub and Rafe found Dora dozing in the water when he went to check on her thirty minutes later. He and Tom bathed next and they all dressed in their best clothes before going to dinner. She was seated beside him at the table, and he squeezed her hand as Edward blessed the food.

After dinner, Dora helped in the kitchen. The men had walked out on the porch to talk. The boys headed to the backyard slamming the screen door behind them. Dora had felt an instant kinship with Mary when they'd met, and as the three women washed dishes together, she asked her about the boys.

"Your boys have your eyes, Mary. The two older ones are about the same size—they're not twins, are they?"

"No, but they're close in age. Eddie and Samuel are just eleven months apart and Harry is two years behind them. They're a handful at times but they're good boys."

Ellie was putting the pans in the cupboard. "They're sure having fun playing together. It's odd isn't it, that among the three of us, we've only boys and no girls?"

Dora fingered the pendant she wore round her neck and thought of little Alice who never had a chance to laugh and play.

Mary dried her hands and put the dish towel away and sighed. Dora looked up to see tears in her eyes. "Ellie, Edward must not have written to Clay about our Rachel. She was only three months old when the cholera took her away two years ago. Samuel had it and he survived. Rachel was a healthy little thing, but the doctor said it hits babies the hardest."

Ellie lifted her hands to her face. "Oh, Mary, I didn't know. I'm so sorry."

Dora reached out and held Mary's hand. "Then our wee ones are in heaven together playing at the feet of Jesus," she said. "Our

Alice has been gone four years now and there's nary a day that I don't think of her. She was born just as pretty a baby as can be, but she never took her first breath."

Mary hugged her. "I knew we were kindred spirits, Dory McCade," she said. "I could sense the same kind of sadness deep within your eyes that I see in mine when I look in a mirror."

The two of them hugged until tears rolled down their cheeks and fell onto each other's shoulders. It felt good to be understood and they knew they would always share this bond even if they never saw each other again.

THE MEN'S conversation on the porch centered around the freight business and the role Clay would play in it. Edward offered Rafe a job and he was speechless when told how much he would be paid. He and Dora and the boy could have a good life in St. Louis and not have to move any farther west.

"It's tempting, Edward," he said. "But Dora's got her head set on going on. And I made a promise to my brother. I sent word before we left home that we would be there by September."

"Talk to Dora. She might like it better here than you think. And you can always write to your brother that you've decided to stay in St. Louis. I'm shorthanded. I was depending on Clay to help me, but he's going to need at least a week's rest. I could use an honest hardworking man and Clay tells me you are both."

"Thank you for that, Clay. I've not let any grass grow under my feet, and my word is as good as any man's. I'll talk to Dora and we'll think it through tonight."

They were lying in bed when Rafe told her about Edward's job offer. "We ain't town people, Rafe. I'd feel cooped up as a snake in a jelly jar if I had to live so close to people. It's a noisy, smelly place and I can't hardly breathe with all the dust and smoke in the air."

"I don't like it either, Dora, but that's a lot of money. Maybe I could work here a year and then we could move on. We'd save enough to buy some cattle when we get to where we're going."

"But that's just it. We might not save much by staying. I overheard Mary telling Ellie about the cost of goods here. Flour is ten dollars a barrel and lard is thirty cents a pound. We paid less than half that back home. I don't see how we can pay those prices and save, do you?"

Rafe looked worried. "And that means we can't buy as much in the way of supplies when we leave."

"We need flour, coffee and lard. And I was hopin' to get some smoked meats."

He put his arm around her and pulled her close. "We can buy it but we'll have to cut back some." He waited a moment and then spoke again. "So, you've a mind to move on then?"

"I'll do whatever you decide, Rafe. The work's bound to be easier than behind a plow on that scraggly farm we had. I don't want to stay here forever though. I keep thinking about those green valleys and creeks running through the Rocky Mountains that Colin told us about in his letters."

Rafe smiled. "Like your hills of Tennessee? You never did like the flat lands of Kentucky, did you?"

"I want to be where you are, Rafe McCade. And if it's here in St. Louis, that's where I'll be."

He held her a little tighter. "But it's smelly and smoky and if it takes the spark out of my woman's eyes, I'll not be having it.

We'll be heading on west as soon as we round up our supplies. It may take another day or two."

She turned to him and snuggled into his arms. "It's good to sleep in a bed in a room all to ourselves, ain't it?" she asked.

His answer was muffled as they drew closer.

"WOULD it be possible for you to stay for just a few more days?" Edward asked when Rafe told him the next morning they would be moving out as soon as they bought supplies. "I just found out that Harley, my warehouse supervisor, was in a bar fight last night and got busted up pretty bad. I've got some cargo to deliver downriver tomorrow. I would get Clay to do it, but he needs to take it easy for a few more days. We'll be gone a few days and if you're willing, I'll hire you to supervise loading the other boat for a shipment to New Orleans. When I return, we'll load up your wagon with supplies and get you on the ferry. It'll take you downstream a few miles where you'll pick up the trail running along the Missouri River to Independence. You'll take the Santa Fe trail from there."

"I'll do it. You can just pay me in supplies if you will."

"You'll be doing me a mighty big favor, Rafe. You've already done me one by keeping my brother from getting killed. I'll buy all the goods you need and pay your wages too."

"IT'S AN ANSWER TO PRAYER, RAFE," Dora said when he walked back inside to tell her. "I was already thinking of ways to stretch our flour and lard. And I'd plumb forgot about cornmeal and molasses."

"Where's Tom this morning?"

"He's showing Mary's boys how to milk Daisy. They're going fishing later unless you got somethin' for him to do."

"No, let him have some fun today. He can work with me the rest of the week and earn his keep."

"I was thinking about that, Rafe. It'll cost Edward and Mary to feed us all week. I think we should pay 'em something, don't you?"

"I don't think Mary would take money, Dora. She'd be nearer to accepting a side of beef or pork. I'll take care of it before we leave."

"I wish she would let me do the cooking and cleaning while we're here."

"Then the maid wouldn't have a job."

"Well, I'm not going to sit around and twiddle my thumbs, I'll tell you that much. If I help that maid clean, her job will be a little easier while we're here."

Rafe smiled at the thought. He'd never seen Dora twiddle her thumbs and didn't think he ever would.

With all the excitement, Rafe and Dora had forgotten all about the reward money. They might not have remembered it at all if the sheriff hadn't paid a visit to Edward's warehouse one morning where Rafe was organizing supplies. Rafe walked out and shook his hand when he saw him coming.

"I heard you were working for Ed this week and didn't want you to run off without your reward money. That feller you brought in was worth every penny of it, and the one you buried was worth even more," he said, handing Rafe the envelope full of money. "This one won't be getting out of jail anytime soon."

When Rafe returned from working that afternoon, he opened the envelope and showed the money to Dora. It was $400.

"I'd do a cartwheel if I thought I could, Rafe," she said. "I feel a right smart better knowing we got a little to put aside and won't be beholding to your brother when we get out there."

Rafe knew they needed the money, but he ached inside for the life he took to get it. They had started off with so little and their money had dwindled. With the reward money and the wages he'd earn by working for Edward, they would be alright.

THERE WERE HUGS, tears and handshaking as the McCades said their goodbyes to the Campbells at the waterfront a week later. Dora had to admit she would miss the company of the women-folk. Ellie, who seemed like a sister she'd never had, and Mary, who shared with her the common bond of grief for the little ones they'd lost.

Edward clasped Rafe's hand as the ferry workers loaded the wagon and horses. "Rafe, If you change your mind when you get to Independence, you can always turn around and come back. You did a fine job while we were gone, and I'd be proud to have a good hand like you."

"I'd be lying if I said I wasn't tempted to stay here in St. Louis. We got rough trails ahead, and I hope we don't regret our decision to go on," he said. "I don't expect we'll be back this way again so I'll tell you now I appreciate all you've done for us, Edward."

Rafe reached for Clay's hand. "And I'm going to miss you, my friend. I wouldn't mind ridin' the whole trail with you."

"Same here," Clay said, shaking his hand warmly. "I'll never be able to repay you for my life, but I'm thankful to be here because of what you did." He looked from Rafe to Ellie. "I don't much think you'll need me anyway. That wife of yours has got spunk and grit and she'll do fine to ride the trail with."

Rafe looked at his wife with pride. "I know. I'm a lucky man."

Log cabins dotted the landscape along the banks of the Missouri River and the McCades watched with interest as they floated downstream on the ferry. Where there were cabins, there were children, and they waved and shouted out greetings to the passengers as they floated by. They were hungry for communication with the outside world in their isolated cabins. It looked like a lonely life and Rafe wondered if he would feel lonely in such a place. At least they would have family where they were going. Colin had been the big brother he always looked up to and he was eager to see him again.

Tom was chatting with a boy about his own age and Dora was watching the world go by with great fascination. Rafe made his way to the wheel where the captain sat. As if reading his mind, the captain nodded and spoke to him. "Another hour if we're lucky. We'll be reaching some shoals around that bend," he said, pointing to a place a short distance away. "If the river's up, we'll have no trouble, but if it's down, we'll need to put out some oars. Either way, we'll get through and you'll have a few more hours of daylight to pick up your trail and be on your way."

That was music to Rafe's ears. They'd spent six days longer than planned in St. Louis. He had some time to make up and was anxious to be on the move again.

"How far will we be from Independence when we dock?" Rafe asked.

"If the weather holds, you can make it in 16 days. Where are you going from there?"

"We'll be picking up the Santa Fe Trail."

"You're not going to Oregon? That's where half the country is headed."

"No, we're heading to New Mexico Territory. My brother has a small spread on the North Platte River, east of the Rockies."

"Is it north or south of Big Sandy Creek?"

"It's on the south end of Big Sandy."

"That's good. Indian's ain't causing much trouble down there these days. About three years ago, it was a different story. The Utes fell out with the Mexicans and were causing all kinds of commotion, but they've settled things as far as I know. You still need to stay clear of the Sioux. I've heard they're stirred up right now, but they generally range north of the Big Sandy."

"I'm not aimin' for Indian trouble."

"Nobody goes looking for it. If they're gonna make trouble, they'll bring it to you. Anyways, it's good you ain't planning on trying to get through the Rockies to Oregon this late in the season."

"Late? July's just begun."

"The Oregon wagon trains are two weeks gone. You don't want no part of the snow in those mountain passes. It can come as early as September."

Rafe pointed ahead. "Looks like the river's up."

"Yeah, we won't need any oars. It won't be long now, and you can be on your way."

And true to the captain's word, within an hour they were on the wagon road to Independence.

CHAPTER SEVEN
A BRIEF RESPITE

Tom's hand shook slightly as he looked down the barrel of his grandpa's Winchester. The buck was unaware that it was being watched as it grazed on the soft summer prairie grass. They had been three days without meat. With only a few pounds of bacon left, Dora was trying to stretch it until they could replenish supplies in Independence. Tom had set traps for rabbits but each time he checked them they were tripped as if someone had already been there before him. But that couldn't be—there was no one within miles of this place or they would have seen signs, his Pa had said. His Ma had laughed and said it must be the Little People living here in the woods as she had heard her Papa speak about from his native Ireland.

Tom had a suspicion that it was Indians as he had found a string with a crude hook tied to a branch down by the creek. Pa said it was more than likely left behind by travelers who had come to this place before them, but he had a worried look when he said it.

"Let's don't be shootin' at nothing," Pa had told him. "Just keep on setting the traps. I'll rig up a trout basket like Ennis taught me to do when I was just a young'un. Why don't you take your slingshot out in the open and see if you can kill a prairie hen. It'll give you something to do and we could use the meat." Trouble was, his slingshot was broken so instead, he grabbed the Winchester from the back of the wagon.

The buck began to move from his grazing place. Tired of biscuits and beans, he watched him move closer and Tom knew the deer would soon get wind of him and run off. He made a quick decision, got him in his sights and pulled the trigger. The buck ran a few yards and dropped.

∼

RAFE HAD JUST FINISHED CHECKING the last of the traps and was puzzling over why they were tripped but empty when he heard the shot. "What's that boy gone and done now?" he muttered to himself. He took off running in the direction of the sound of the gunshot.

Tom was standing over the buck when Rafe got there.

"Good shot, boy."

Tom looked up and blushed when he saw Rafe. "Papa, I know you told me not to shoot but that deer was begging for it."

"What's done is done," Rafe said. "No use worrying over it. We need the meat—the traps came up empty again."

Rafe and Tom both took their knives out and started cutting through the belly of the deer. They worked quietly for a while and then Rafe stopped.

"Just take what we can use without it spoiling," Rafe said. "We'll be leaving come morning and we won't have time to smoke much of the meat. This'll last us for a few days. We'll take the hide and tan it along the way."

Rafe was careful to leave some of the good cuts of meat. Someone was close by, he had no doubt, and they were either weak or hurt. The empty traps told their own tale.

TOM'S MOUTH watered as he smelled the roasting venison on the spit. As Dora was preparing the meal, Rafe had started scraping the deer hide after soaking it for a few hours in the creek. "I've changed my mind. We'll stay here one more day before movin' on," he said. "We need more time for this hide. It'll need to be soaked again, and it's best to do it while it's fresh."

Tom was watching Rafe work on the hide. "Pa, what'll happen to the meat we left back yonder?"

Rafe kept his head lowered as he worked. He didn't want to lie to the boy, but he didn't want to scare him either. "More'n likely coyotes will have a feast on it tonight." Tom turned back to the fire and Dora caught Rafe's eye.

Dora was concerned. She knew Rafe would never put tanning a hide ahead of moving on. There was more to it than that. With a shiver born of superstition, she suddenly decided it would be best if they were shuck o' this place. They'd had a good rest and the deer Tom shot was a Godsend. It was the best meat they'd had in a while. She had cut some thin strips and left them beside the fire to smoke overnight along with some wild onions that Tom found growing along the edge of the prairie grass. Game had been scarce and smoked jerky would be fine eating compared to biscuits and beans. Dried onions would help tenderize and flavor a stew made from the tougher cuts of meat.

When they finished eating, Tom carried the bucket down to the creek to get water. While he was there, he checked the traps again, but none were tripped. He lifted his trotline out of the creek and baited the hooks with bits of gristle from the deer in hopes of catching some fish. Pa told him it wasn't much use, but it wouldn't hurt to try. Ma sure would be surprised if he caught a mess of fish for breakfast. Satisfied that the line would hold, he slowly dropped each hook into the water, then crawled back up the creekbank. He picked up the water bucket and started walking back to the camp. He heard a faint rustling sound and stopped to listen. When he didn't hear it again, he picked up his pace. If there was a bear around, they would have seen signs of it, but it was dark and the sound spooked him enough that he was glad to see the glow of the fire when he stepped into the clearing of their camp.

"You were gone a good while," Rafe said, looking the boy over.

"I checked on the traps. They're still set." He poured the bucket of water in the kettle over the fire to heat up for washing the supper dishes.

"Did you see anything?" Rafe asked.

"No, but I heard a rustling out there," he said. "Probably a rabbit. Or it could have been that skunk we smelled last night."

"More'n likely", Rafe said, keeping his eyes on his work as he scraped away at the hide.

"If it's a rabbit, maybe it'll get caught in one of our traps tonight."

"Think I'll turn in now," Tom said, heading to the back of the wagon.

"Good idea. I'll wake you up when it's your turn to watch."

Dora frowned. They were in a good secluded place and not much reason to post a watch at night. There were other good places they had camped where they'd all slept through the night along the way. She shivered again. When the water was hot, she poured it into the wash pan and made short work of cleaning up the dishes. She dried them and put them back in the hinged box Rafe had built on the side of the wagon. While he was working on the deer hide, she reached in the back of the wagon for her hairbrush and then joined him at the fire.

"What is it you're worryin' over, Rafe?"

When he didn't answer, she didn't push him—she knew he had something on his mind and would answer when he'd thought it out. She took the pins out of her hair and let it fall loose from the bun she wore during the day. After she worked the tangles out with the boar-bristle brush, her long red hair shone like copper in the firelight.

She loved watching Rafe work. He was scraping the last bits of flesh from the hide and would soak it again tomorrow. He would then salt it down and let it dry out. In the days ahead, he would work with the hide, stretching it to make it more pliable. Later, she would sew it into a shirt or jacket. She had watched her father and brothers tan many hides as they sat by a warm fire on cold winter nights.

"You're awful quiet," she said finally.

Rafe looked up and grinned. "You mean to say I'm usually noisy?"

She didn't say anything but looked at him intently. He squirmed. "You can read me like a book, Dora. I can't rightly say what's bothering me, though. It's just a feeling I got." He looked back down at the hide he was scraping. "I don't think we're in any danger, but I'm puzzled." He pointed to his gun at his side, "but just in case, I got the shotgun handy. I'll keep working on this for a while. It'll keep me from getting sleepy."

She stared at him a moment, loving the way his eyes smiled along with the rest of his face. They were kind eyes, although they were usually hidden beneath his shaggy brows, and she wondered again at how lucky she was to have got such a good man, and a right handsome one to boot. His face was a mite thin and angular, but he had a strong chin and she'd always admired a strong chin. She had been born poor as Job's turkey in the hills of Tennessee and her only learnin' had come from life's hard knocks. Rafe, on the other hand, had gone to school till he was nigh on twelve years old. She trusted her man and felt relief that he didn't feel they were in any danger. That was something, at least. She knew Rafe would tell her the truth, no matter if it did scare her. It was something he had promised her before they started out. She finished brushing her hair and got up from the stool. She took a soft cloth and wet it in the still warm water in the pot and washed her face and neck, then turned to the wagon again. "I think I'll turn in too," she said. "Give me a holler if you need me."

Rafe worked on the hide a little while longer until the fire had burned down to just glowing embers. He took Dora's stool with him and made as if he was going to the back of the wagon, but instead, he slipped off a few yards away into the brush and sat on the stool to keep watch. The night was warm and the only sounds he heard were the night noises—the cicadas and the occasional call of a whip-poor-will. After a while, he grew sleepy and nodded off.

The sound of a twig breaking woke him up with a start and he looked around. The black of night had yielded to a soft, but still dark gray sky. It looked to be about an hour before daylight. There was a shadow of someone near the cold ashes of the fire. A thief, apparently trying to find something else to steal. He felt the anger well up in him. Whoever it was just couldn't be content with stealing from his traps. Nor were they content with the meat he'd left for them. Well, they weren't going to get away with stealing right under his nose in his very own camp, no siree!

He stood up quietly, then made up his mind to go full speed around the wagon and tackle whoever it was before they could be warned. He took off running and was surprised when he grabbed someone that felt light as a shuck o' corn. He held on tight to the arm that wasn't half the size of Dora's, and even though it fought like a wildcat, he didn't have any trouble subduing it until something suddenly bit him on the shoulder.

"Ouch!" he hollered. "Cut that out! Dora, get out here with the lantern, will ya?"

Tom came out the front of the wagon with the lantern lit in his hand, and Dora stayed out of sight in the wagon, holding the rifle. "Why, it's just a slip of a girl," Dora said with surprise. "An Indian girl, at that."

The girl jerked her arm, trying to get loose again, but Rafe held on tight. When the girl saw Dora come out, she relaxed a little, but her dark eyes were still filled with fear. Dora put the rifle on the seat of the wagon next to Tom and hopped down.

"Come on child, nobody's gonna hurt you," she said, soothingly. "What in tarnation are you doin' out here all alone anyway?"

The girl didn't answer. "Could be she's not alone," Tom said, putting the lantern down on the seat and picking up his rifle. The girl tensed up again when she saw the rifle and tried once again to get out of Rafe's grip.

"Put that gun down, boy. Don't you know you're scaring her to death?" Dora sat down on the log where Rafe had been stripping the hide the night before. The sky had lightened enough to see that the girl couldn't have been over twelve or thirteen, close to the age of Tom, but not nearly as big. "Rafe, bring her here. You're making her skittery."

He brought her over and shoved her down on the log. "You're welcome to her. She bites like a wildcat."

"Don't be so rough on the child," Dora scolded. She held onto the girls arm firmly. "She'll settle down soon and we'll see if we can find out what she's doing here."

Tom had jumped down from the wagon and was looking around. "What's this?" he asked, picking up a basket that had fallen to the ground in the scuffle.

Rafe walked over and took it from Tom. "It's filled with nuts and berries."

Tom was busy on the ground, picking up some that had fallen out. "Here's some dandelion greens and roots too."

Rafe held out the basket to the girl. She shook her head and pointed at the basket, then at Rafe, Tom, and Dora.

"Pa, I think she wants to pay us back for the meat you left out there in the draw today."

"Yeah, and maybe the traps she stole from, too," Rafe said, still leery of the girl sitting on the log with Dora. "We better be careful. Where there's one Indian, there's more," he said. "There ain't no way this mite of a young'un could eat all that food she's been stealing."

"I don't call it stealin' if she was trying to pay us back with what's in this basket. Tom, you bank up the fire, and Rafe, you put some coffee on," Dora ordered. She still held onto the girl's arm, but more gently. "We'll wait until daylight and have her lead us to her camp."

"They might be setting us up," Rafe said, but he went about helping Tom stoke up the fire. The young girl finally gave up her struggles and leaned her head onto Dora's shoulder. In a matter of minutes, the warmth from the fire had lulled her into a sound sleep.

"You get some sleep, Pa. I'll take my turn at watch now."

"Rafe smiled. "I slept through my watch, Son. You go on back to your tent. It's not long to daybreak, but you might get in a few winks." He looked over at his wife and saw that the young Indian girl had stretched out on the log with her head in Dora's lap. He caught her eye and she smiled.

"She's all tuckered out," she whispered. "I wonder where her folks are?" She looked down at the girl tenderly and smoothed her long silky hair away from her face.

"Probably sittin' back in the woods watching us, but it looks like I would have seen signs by now if there's many of 'em. We'll take a look when it gets light enough to see. Maybe we can get her to talk."

"Wouldn't do any good if she did," Dora said. "None of us know the talk of the Indians out here in this neck of the woods. There were some Cherokee up in the hills back home and I learned their words playing in the woods with 'em. They were friendly folk and would bring us a deer or a wild turkey when my daddy was too sick to do any huntin'. Old Andrew Jackson rounded 'em up a few years back and herded 'em westward, pert-near killed 'em too from what I heard. Heard some folks callin' it a trail of tears. Could be she's from a band of Cherokee, you think?"

"Could be," Rafe said, "but that was years ago, and they took to a trail further south than ours. She's more than likely a Pawnee. We'll find out when she wakes up." He watched Dora as she shifted to make the girl more comfortable. He jumped up and came round to the log they were sitting on. "Here, let me settle the girl on a blanket. Your back's bound to be hurting sitting up straight like that."

"No, I'm alright. I don't want to startle her. She must not have been getting much sleep if she was raiding your traps every night." She raised her eyes to meet Rafe's. "That was decent of her to bring us nuts and berries, wadn't it?"

"I suppose it was," Rafe said, yawning. "I just wish I knew where the rest of them were hiding out. They might not be so friendly when they see us with the girl."

THE RED-TINGED SKY to the east signaled the beginning of a new day, and already the smell of johnny cakes cooking in the black iron skillet wafted in the air and into the senses of the man leaning against the wagon. Rafe stirred, then opened his eyes and jumped up, almost knocking the water barrel off the wagon.

"Shh," Dora whispered, nodding her head in the direction of the log. "She's still sleeping." But it was too late, the commotion had awakened the girl and she jumped with a start and sat up. Dora dropped the crudely made spatula in the skillet and ran over to the girl. "Don't let them burn, Rafe, or we won't be having breakfast."

As she soothed the frightened child, Rafe stumbled to the fire and flipped the cakes over to sizzle on the other side. "Here now," she said soothingly. "Everything's gonna be alright." The young girl's eyes were wide with fear, but she finally settled down.

"You've got a way with young'ins," Rafe said. "See if she can talk."

Dora pointed to her own mouth, then pointed to the girl's. "Talk?" The girl shook her head. Dora made a hand-puppet motion with her hand, moving it up and down, and once again asked, "Talk?" Another shake of the head. Rafe watched with amusement.

"I reckon she's got nothing to say," he said, grinning.

"Siyo," Dora said, followed by a string of strange sounding words that didn't make a lick of sense to Rafe. "Tsalagi tsiwoni."

The girl's eyes brightened, and she talked back in the same language.

"Cherokee," Dora exclaimed in delight. "And I think she trusts us since I can speak her language."

"Ask her if she's alone."

Dora took her time and puzzled over some of the words, but the girl seemed to understand and talked back, when not with words, then with her hands. Rafe saw her point toward the creek, then she started walking, pulling at Dora's skirt. "She says her enisi is sick. That's either her grandfather or grandmother, I can't remember which, but she said she'd lead us there," Dora said, motioning to Rafe. "Come on, now."

"Let's eat first. The cakes are warm, and it's been a long night. There's no tellin' what we'll find when we get there. We might be walking into a trap and if we do, I'd rather have a full stomach."

Tom came out of the back of the wagon, yawning and wiping at his eyes. "I see she's still here. Where'd she come from?" he asked.

Dora poured up some coffee and put the johnny cakes on the tin plates. "We don't rightly know," she said. "But we'll soon be finding out. She's going to lead us to where she's staying but your pa wants to eat first."

They ate hurriedly; the girl ate hungrily and before they left, Rafe turned to Tom. "Stay and guard the wagon, son. I don't 'spect trouble, but you never know. Your ma and I will be back shortly."

"Wait," Dora said, and headed back to the campfire. "Whoever is waitin' for this girl to get back is hungry too. I'll leave you a few to snack on later, Tom, but I'll take the rest with us."

Rafe's face fell. "What about me?"

"Don't fret over it, Rafe. I'll make more tomorrow."

RAFE FIGURED the copse of trees where they'd spent the last couple of days covered about twenty square acres. It was mostly flat except for a steep cliff of rocks near the creek bed. He thought he'd combed every inch of it when their traps kept coming up empty, trying to find someone or something that had been springing them. He had discounted the rocks since they looked to be too sheer to climb, but the girl led them down into the creek bed, and from that side of the rock, there was a small trail that wasn't hard at all to climb. When they got to the top, there were hollows in the rock where ten to twelve people could hide out, but there was only an old Indian man wrapped up in a blanket half-sitting with another blanket as a pillow against the rock. Another shelf of rocks above formed a cave-like shelter. It was a perfect hiding place to protect him and the girl from the elements. A look of relief flooded the eyes of the old man when he saw the girl, and there was no fear in him as he watched Rafe and Dora come closer.

"You friend," he said, not as a question but as a statement, "or girl would not bring you here." The young girl started talking to him in their native tongue and pointed to Dora. He looked at Dora. "How is it you speak Cherokee?"

"I was raised in the hills to the east of here," she said. "We lived alongside the Cherokee until they were uprooted and pushed west. There were some who stayed in the hills and my Pa helped hide 'em out. I learned to speak some. How is it you speak our language?"

The old man smiled. "Same. I too lived in hills. I had many paleface friends." His smile turned into a scowl. "Not now. Paleface tricked Cherokee and made us leave. Many of my people die on the trail."

Dora looked at him with sympathy. "It wasn't those of us who lived among you. It was old Andy Jackson. He didn't like Indians. Your people were good people. My family had many Cherokee friends."

Rafe pointed at Dora, then at himself. "We are your friends. Why are you not with your tribe?"

With Dora's prodding, the old man finally got the story out. The land where the Cherokee and other tribes were forced to live was over-hunted and the chief took a small band farther north to find game. The young girl had followed her grandfather without their knowledge. When she caught up to them, it was too late to send her back. After a few days of hunting, they ran into an army patrol. The soldiers drew their weapons thinking the Indians had purposely left the Indian Territory to steal and plunder as some other tribes had done. If frightened the Cherokee so they ran and the "old one" was hit by a bullet.

He pointed to his injured leg. "Soldier's bullet."

The patrol followed but the Indians lost them. They came upon the woods and made camp. The warriors had gone to hunt food and left the old Indian and the girl to tend to him but so far they had not returned.

"They don't come back—many nights now." He pulled a stick from underneath the deer hide he'd been resting on and showed it to Dora. It was carved with deep grooves and she counted them.

"Fifteen notches," she said. "Fifteen days they've been gone. Your men must'a run into some trouble. It's a wonder you didn't starve."

He pointed to his granddaughter with the stick. "The girl caught fish and picked berries."

Rafe mumbled under his breath. "And stole from our traps."

Dora gave him a scathing look. "Shush, she tried to make up for it."

The old man's attention went back to the stick and he ran his fingers over the notches and shook his head. "Too many nights come and go. Maybe soldiers take my people back to the place of sickness and hunger. I go no more. Agawel a sga," he said, pausing again. Then he pointed to himself. "Old man. I have lived many moons, but girl—she go with you."

The girl started crying softly, "vtla, enisi, no!"

Dora looked at Rafe. "She calls him grandfather and tells him no she's not leaving him."

"We'll carry you in our wagon," Rafe said to the chief. "Maybe we'll come upon some of your people."

The old man shook his head. "No," he said emphatically. "If soldiers find me in your wagon, you will be punished for hiding me. You take her." He pointed to the child. "She Chenoa. They will not know she is my granddaughter."

"Chenoa is her name?" Dora asked. The man nodded.

"Dove," she said. She looked at the girl and smiled.

"White Dove," the old Indian said. "Take her with you. I die here with this." He pointed to a colorful sash woven with gold thread and elaborate beadwork. "Not afraid to die."

Rafe knew it was the sash of an honored chief. Something had happened to the group they traveled with. The Cherokee would never leave such an honored man if they didn't plan to return for him. Maybe the chief was right. There would likely be trouble if they tried to take him along, but they would honor the chief's wishes and take the girl.

Dora knelt beside the old man. His skin was weathered, and his eyes were dark and hard to read. His shirt was made of deer hide and he wore a necklace made of quills, tiny shells and beads with a round copper medallion in the center. She had seen such medallions hammered out of copper in the Cherokee village near her parents' cabin back in Eastern Tennessee and she wondered if his people might have been her neighbors.

The left leg of his pants was torn up above the knee and the wound was visible.

"Is the bullet still in there?" she asked.

"No, I cut it out."

Dora knew it was no easy feat for a person to remove a bullet from their own self. He was a tough old Indian. The wound was red and swollen and needed to be cleaned and drained.

She opened the flour sack and handed him one of the warm johnny cakes. "Here, eat this." He ate it quickly and she gave him another.

Standing back up, Dora motioned to Rafe. "We need to talk."

Rafe grinned at her. "Go ahead, Dora. Nothin's ever stopped you before."

"No," she said, "over there." She nodded her head to the left. "Alone." She handed the cakes to the young girl who sat down beside her grandfather. He ate them ravenously as she watched. Rafe followed Dora to the far corner of the rock. There was a natural rock shelf where smoked meat and fish were drying on a rack made of twigs.

"So, this is why my traps were empty," he said. He was impressed with the child's ability to preserve food and couldn't help but admire her.

Dora was focused on the situation at hand. "We can't leave the old Indian here, Rafe. He's a chief."

"He says he's dying, Dora. We have to honor his wishes."

"He's not dying. His leg's hurt bad but that's all that's wrong. He's trying to protect the girl and get her out of here before something happens. But without her, he's got no way to get food."

"Dora, the man said so himself. If the soldiers catch us hiding a renegade Cherokee, we'll be in trouble."

"He's not a renegade. You heard him; they were just hunting for food."

"The army doesn't know that. He's got food here and we can leave him some of our traps to use when he runs out."

"What good would that do? He can't walk. Did you see how bad his leg is infected? It needs to be cleaned and dressed regularly."

Rafe groaned inwardly. What were they getting themselves into? When Dora made up her mind, nothing could stop her. He looked in her eyes and could see the determination. "We'll talk about it when the time comes," he said. At least he could put her off for now.

"Could you fetch my medicine bag out of the wagon?" she asked, dismissing any further discussion. "And I'll need some boiling water."

"What else?" he asked as he walked away because he knew she wasn't done with him yet.

"The willowbark," she said. "Tom knows where it is."

He stopped and turned around. "I'll get it. We can build a fire here on the rock to boil the water."

"Take the girl with you. She can help gather sticks for the fire and gather some wild onions. She'll find some growing in the clearing near our camp."

"If she'll go."

"She'll go. The chief likes us, though I don't know why with all the wrongs we've done to the Cherokee."

"We didn't do it, Dora. It was done by other men."

"We're white, ain't we?" she asked, putting her hands on her hips. "That's enough to make them not trust us."

"I think he's smart enough to know the difference. He knows there's good and bad in white people; just like we know there's good and bad in Indians. Some people think they're all savages."

~

WITH THE FIRE going strong and the pot of water boiling, Dora set about cleaning the injured leg. The old man didn't utter a sound, but she could see the pain in his eyes. When she finished, she took her mortar and pestle from the bag, added leaves and petals from two drawstring bags and began to crush them. She added hot water to the mixture to make tea. While it was cooling she took a piece of cloth from her bag and dipped it into the boiling water several times, then fit it over the top of a tin pan where the willowbark and onion were beginning to soften.

"Use this cheesecloth to drain the water out of the willowbark, Rafe, and make a poultice for his leg. But don't throw the water out." She looked around the makeshift camp the Cherokees had made on the rock. "We don't want to waste it. Pour it in that clay bowl." She motioned to the girl. "Chenoa, fetch that bowl over here." The girl understood well enough and did as Dora asked.

While Rafe was making the poultice, Dora took the cup of hot tea and sat down beside the old man. "Drink this. It'll take some of the pain and fever out'a you."

He eyed it suspiciously. He smelled it, then gave her a questioning look.

"It's made from leaves and petals of the Meadowsweet plant," she said. "It grows in the wet places back in the hills. I brought some seeds with me when Rafe became my man and planted them along the crick that runs alongside our farm. Good medicine."

He took a sip, then nodded his head again. "Good medicine," he agreed, and drank the rest from the cup. Rafe brought the hot poultice over and with tender care, Dora placed it on top of the open wound. The old man flinched as the hot cloth burned into his flesh, but he didn't utter a sound. He leaned back against the rock as she pressed it to his leg and tied it in place with two strips of cloth.

"Chief, you listen up now," she said. "Tell the girl to heat the willowbark milk back up later and pour some over the poultice. It'll draw the infection out. Keep doing it a little bit at a time until it's gone. We ain't leaving out today. I'll check up on you before dark and make you up another batch." She went through the motions of what the girl was to do until they both understood. "I'll send our boy up here with some food later on."

The old chief beckoned Rafe to come over. "Sit," he commanded. Rafe looked up at Dora and she nodded.

"Does he want to smoke a peace pipe or something?" Rafe asked before he made any moves.

"He wants to look you in the eye. The Cherokee size up a man by his eyes, so don't look down or over at me. Look straight into his eyes." Rafe wasn't so sure but he walked over and sat cross-legged in front of the chief. Dora stood aside and listened.

"Your woman walks medicine path like Indian. Makes good medicine. Good medicine woman. Her man will live a long life." He picked up his sash from the stone slab and motioned to Rafe. "You keep woman, or you trade?"

Rafe wanted to laugh but saw how serious the chief was and didn't make light of his words. He nodded. "Yes, good medicine, good woman. I keep my woman."

The old man nodded and put the sash back down. "I sleep now. Go."

Dora blushed at the chief's words. She got up first and picked up the medicine bag from the rock, leaving the things she would need later and started climbing down to the creekbed. Rafe was right behind her. When they reached the ground and started walking on the mossy path, he stopped and looked around. Dora stopped too. "What's wrong?" she asked.

"I was just thinking I should go back," he said.

"Why, did you leave something?"

There was a glint in his eye. "There was some mighty fancy beadwork in that sash."

She slapped him on the arm, but a small smile spread across her face. "Could be the chief's wrong. My man mightn't be living so long at all."

Rafe put his arm around her and they walked side by side back to the camp. "Good medicine woman," he said, and kissed her on top of the head. Dora was right. He'd already taken the life of one man and if he left the chief here without his granddaughter, he would be causing the death of another.

THE SETTING SUN was casting shadows through the woods and into the little clearing where they'd made camp. The prairie grass beyond had been shimmering gold throughout the afternoon. Now, the glimmer filtering through the branches of the trees looked for all the world like dancing shadows to Tom. "Don't we need to be movin' on?" he asked as they were eating dinner. "This place spooks me."

"Let's figure it out in the morning," Dora said. "The chief's leg wasn't quite so feverish when I put a new poultice on it this afternoon." She looked at Rafe with concern. "What are we going to do? We can't just leave him to starve."

Rafe looked at his wife fondly. She was always worrying over others with no regard for herself. "Don't worry, Dora. We'll see what tomorrow brings. With your doctorin', he's liable to be up and running around before this night is over."

She looked to the westward sky. "That cloud over yonder is aimin' to be a rainmaker," she said. "I don't want to be stuck here if it's gonna rain more'n a day or two. We may have to take him with us for a spell until his leg heals."

"We'll do what needs to be done," Rafe said. He turned to Tom who was busy sopping his biscuit in the gravy Dora had made from the fried deer steak drippings. "You better be gatherin' more wood for the fire afore it gets dark."

"I already did," Tom said. "It's stacked behind the wagon."

Rafe nodded his head and looked steadily at his son. "I'm seein' you shaping up to be a man right before my eyes."

Tom held his gaze and tried not to show the pleasure his Pa's words had given him. "Yes sir, I'm tryin'."

Dora yawned as they sat by the fire after supper. "I think I'll turn in."

"Go on, then. I'll stay here and keep the fire burnin'."

"Will you be sleeping in the tent tonight?" she asked. "Since most of our stuff is under the lean-to, there's plenty of room in the wagon."

"I think I'll stay outside in case the Indians come back for the girl and the chief," he said. "Besides, it's too hot to be cooped up inside."

"Yeah, it's a right sticky night and not a breeze a'stirring. Tom? How about you?"

"I'll stay out here with Pa." He started to rise from the log where he was sitting. "I'll get my blanket from the wagon."

"Keep your seat. I'll throw it out to you."

Dora was the first one up and about. Tom had crawled into his tent sometime during the night but Rafe stuck it out and was asleep on his blanket under the wagon. She didn't blame him much; the stifling heat had caused her to toss and turn for the first hour or two after she'd gone to bed. It was Tom's job to milk the cow, but since she was awake before daybreak, she decided to let him sleep a little longer. She nudged her foot against Rafe's shin. It startled him and he sat up straight, banging his head against the undercarriage. She laughed.

"I didn't mean to scare you—just wanted you to know I'm up and stirrin' about."

He grinned. "I know you better than that, Dora. It's the mischief you got in you from your Black Irish blood. What if it had been a leprechaun you'd be kicking in the shin?"

Dora gave him a hard look, but he could see the hint of a smile and knew what she was up to. "There'll be no talk of wee leprechauns. The devil himself will have ye in chains before the day is up and may ye be at the gates of heaven an hour before he knows ye are dead." She whisked her skirt at him and took the stool and the milk bucket down from a hook on the wagon. "Off with you to build up the fire and put the coffee on to boil. I'll be milking Daisy as the sun comes up on this fine and glorious morn."

Rafe rolled up his blanket and put it back in the wagon. He loved it when she drifted her speech into the playful Irish lilt of her ancestors. He'd been concerned before they began their journey that she wouldn't be up for it, but not anymore. They were a tough lot, those Irish. He had the blood of the Irish himself, but only from his Pa whereas Dora got a double wallop of it from both her parents. He pitied the person who tried to take advantage of his woman. He'd made a good choice in a bride. As she had already proved, she was one to be reckoned with.

TRUE TO HER prediction of a fine and glorious morn. The storm had missed them and the sky was a marvel to behold as Dora walked to where Daisy was staked out on the prairie grass. Soft muted colors of lavender, pink and peach tinged the wispy clouds on the eastern horizon and the sun's first rays were shining brilliantly up into the air above.

She put the stool on Daisy's right flank and the bucket under her teats. She sat down and talked softly to the cow. "I see you've been grazin' on milk-vetch this morning, Daisy girl. That'll make for some fine-tasting milk."

In one of their camps, Tom had come in with the milk bucket one morning and Dora had made up a batch of biscuits and poured them all a cup of milk to drink with their breakfast. Tom took the first swig and made a wry face. "What's Daisy been into?" he asked, spitting it out on the ground. Rafe took a drink. "Garlic", he said. "It won't hurt you none. Go ahead and drink it." To prove his point, he drained his cup, but his wrinkled-up nose told the real story. The biscuits had a slight off-taste but when they slathered them with honey, they were edible. Since the Campbells had lost their milk cow, they'd been extra careful where they staked the cow at night but they hadn't noticed the wild garlic growing on the hillside.

As Dora milked Daisy, her eyes scoured the area for other plants. The wildflowers were abundant, and she wished she knew more about the medicinal purposes for the plants in this region. She spotted a patch of phlox which was said to be good for cleansing the blood. When she finished her milking, she moved Daisy to another patch of grass to graze making sure the cow was well-hidden from any dishonest folks who might come along the trail. Some wild peppermint was growing on the creek bank. Mint leaves worked well for pain and infection, so she gathered some. She put the mint and the phlox into her apron and started back with the stool and the milk pail. Just as she reached the trees, she heard the sound of horses, so she ducked under cover just in time before a small band of soldiers came into view. She hurried back to the camp knowing it would be a matter of minutes before they smelled the campfire and came back. Rafe had heard them too. He had brought up the last of the fresh venison from the cool spring water and was frying it up in the iron skillet.

"Soldiers," she said. "Seven or eight of 'em."

"Just act natural," he said. "I'm sure the Indians heard them too, as much noise as they made coming through. They'll stay hidden. I got plenty of meat to offer 'em if they've a mind to eat. It needed cooking anyway before it spoilt."

"I'll make up a batch of biscuits, or do you think I should do fritters?"

"Make the fritters. We've got more cornmeal than flour. It'll be faster too. The sooner we get shuck of 'em, the better off we'll be."

Dora looked around. "Where's Tom?"

"He's lookin' the traps. He's been gone long enough he should be back by now."

They heard a noise and Tom came from behind the wagon. "I'm back," he said. He was holding a rabbit by its hind feet. "It's alive," he said. "It got caught in the snare I made yesterday. Should I kill it?"

"No, let it live and put it inside Ma's basket. It's so hot today, I'm afraid the meat will spoil before supper if we dress it out now. The only place cold enough is at the spring head where the chief and the girl are, and I don't want you going there. We'll be having some visitors shortly."

"I know. I've already been there. White Dove was looking for some medicine plants and I ran into her," he said. "We heard the horses, and she took care to wipe out our tracks to the rock and the water below. She's a smart one. She sure threw us off, didn't she?"

"It doesn't take much to fool us greenhorns with Indian tricks," Rafe said, "but these soldiers are a whole lot better at tracking. We'll have to be mighty persuasive to convince them there aren't any Indians around here."

Dora had whipped up the batter for the fritters and was heating up another skillet while Rafe tended to the venison. She turned to Tom. "Me and your Pa don't cotton to tellin' lies, but we don't want to get those two in trouble either. We don't know what kind of people those soldiers are yet. There's good and there's bad in all of us and I don't want no bad getting ahold of that old man and little girl. They put their trust in us, and we've got to honor it. That means we need to throw those soldiers off the scent of White Dove and the chief. There's lying for the sake of lying, and there's hiding the truth for the sake of protecting someone. I want you to know the difference, son."

Tom nodded his head. "Yes ma'am. I do."

Just as the first batch of fritters dropped into the pan, the horses rode into camp. Dora pretended she was startled and splashed grease from the pan onto her arm. "Ouch," she cried out.

The captain had a revolver drawn but holstered it when he dismounted. "Sorry ma'am. I didn't mean to frighten you. We smelled the smoke and didn't know what we might be getting into."

Dora dipped her finger in the can of lard and layered it on her arm. "You ought to be ashamed, scaring us like that," she said. "You caused me to burn my arm and are liable to cause me to burn our breakfast."

"Like I said, ma'am, I'm sorry." He scooped off his hat and bowed. "Captain McCullum at your service, ma'am."

"Well at least you're an Irish lad!" she said. "You can't be all bad. I've got a bit of the Irish blood in meself." She reached for the spatula and turned the fritters. "Could it be you boys are hankerin' after some fritters?" She batted her long eyelashes at them and smiled. "I've got a big batch of 'em a'fryin'. If you've got something to eat off of, you can share our food. We don't have extra plates."

Hats came off as the soldiers scrambled to dismount and pull their tin plates out of their mess kits, each man eager for a morsel of food prepared by the hands of a lady and a stirring of warm memories of mothers or wives putting food on the table before them. Rafe smiled to himself. What a resourceful woman he'd married. She had put one of her Irish spells on them already. Hells bells—she'd said she couldn't manage without him but he knew if something happened to him she could and she would. It gave him peace of mind, it surely did!

～

"CHEROKEES!" Dora exclaimed. "Why would they be here?" she asked while the men were devouring their breakfast. Each question the captain asked, Dora parlayed with another question instead of answering with a lie.

"They've broken away from the land they were assigned to," Captain McCullum answered. "It's a renegade bunch run by a fierce old chief."

"Are they to be feared?" Dora asked with wide eyes.

A lad who looked no older than twenty shuffled his feet. "Not likely. The chief is old and food has been scarce. They're going hungry on the reservation." His voice had the distinct twang of a fellow Tennessean, and Dora looked at him with interest, but the sergeant in the small band of soldiers gave him a scathing look.

"Our duty is to bring them back, Private Taylor, not to concern ourselves over their food shortages."

"Yes, Sir," he said, looking a little put-out.

"There'll be no arguing over our duties," Captain McCullum said, "and no troubling these folks any longer." He stood up and rinsed his army issued tin plate and cup in Dora's dishwater and motioned to his men to do the same. After they packed them in their saddlebags, they stood at attention while the Captain said his goodbyes.

We'll be on our way, Mrs. McCade, and we thank you for your hospitality." He tipped his hat to Rafe. "Tis a fine cook ye've got here, Mr. McCade. We'll be remembering the fine eating for many a day." As he lifted his foot into the stirrup, he called out to his men, "Mount up! We're movin' on." There was a rush to put hats back on and a scurry to get their seats in the saddles.

"Top o' the day to ye," the Captain said. A scattering of "thank you, ma'ams" was heard throughout the group of men and they moved out in an orderly fashion.

"Do you think they believed us?" Tom asked as the last of them turned out.

"There was nothing we said that would cause 'em not to believe. The way your Ma turned their questions right back at 'em, they merely surmised that no Indians were about. If she'd told an outright lie, it might have given them pause to wonder. Not many people can stand up to the scrutiny of having told a lie. Something always gives it away and it's usually the eyes. Hard to look someone in the eyes when you're lying."

Tom grinned. "Like the time I told you I milked Daisy and I didn't?"

"It weren't your eyes that gave you away that time," he said with a grin. "It was the empty bucket."

"And old Daisy's sack was still full," Tom said, grinning. "That was a pretty dumb story to tell. I was just shamed I hadn't milked her like you told me to."

Rafe nodded his head. "And you learned right quick that it bothered me a whole heap more that you told a lie."

"I wasn't old enough to know how to tell a proper lie," Tom said with a mischievous look in his eye. He ducked when Rafe pretended to cuff his ear. "And I don't recall tellin' one again. You burned me good with a switch—I do remember that."

"It was a good thing to learn, Tom. And it was a good way your ma explained it too. A boy who tells lies doesn't shape up to be much of a man."

"Y'all just keep jabbering," Dora said as she took off her apron. "I'll get my medicine bag and go check on the chief." She grabbed up the peppermint and put it in the bag. "If you hurry and clean up this mess, you can go with me. We'll decide what to do when we see how his leg is healing."

Rafe scraped the bits of meat off the griddle and left it soaking in the dishwater while Tom dried the clean utensils and put them back in the crate. Dora stepped out of the wagon with her satchel. "I'll finish cleaning the griddle when we get back," Rafe said. "Come along now, Tom. We'll pick up some sticks to build a fire when we get there."

"No need," Dora said. "I've got hot water in the kettle. Rafe, will you tote it?"

"I will," he said. "It's too hot for you to carry."

"And heavy," she said.

Rafe touched the handle to be sure it was cool enough to handle before he lifted the kettle from the coals.

Dora picked up a towel she'd put aside. Wrapped up inside were some of the fritters and the leftover venison. "The chief and the girl will be hungry. If I hadn't hid these, those men would have gobbled 'em up. You'd a' thought they hadn't seen food in a month of Sundays."

"Food always tastes better from the hands of a woman," Rafe said. "They've been away from their camp for some days now and I'd say they've had slim pickings."

Dora turned to Tom. "Did you see the chief this morning?"

"Not yet. I was on my way to see him when we heard the horses, so I rushed back."

"We'll find out soon enough," she said, and scuttled up ahead of them.

The old chief was sitting up when the McCades climbed up to their hiding place. Dora took the bandage off and was pleased to see the girl had done her own tending to the wound. The poultice was different and looked to have been applied early this morning. Dora looked at it carefully, then looked at the girl.

"Where did you find this?" she asked. It was something different from the meadowsweet plant she'd used the day before. The girl pointed to the creek bank. Dora nodded. "So, you know a little bit about medicine too. That's good." She pulled the poultice back.

The chief nodded. "My son was a medicine man. He and his woman died of sickness."

"White Dove's ma and pa?" Dora asked.

The chief nodded.

"What kind of sickness?" she asked.

"White man sickness."

"Could be a number of things," Dora said, turning to Rafe, "but I figure it was Cholera. We brought more grief to the Indian people than just stealing their land. We brought our diseases."

Rafe nodded. "What kind of plant did the girl use for the poultice?"

"Yarrow. It's good for wounds. She must have seen her father use plants."

The chief spoke up. "He used many plants."

"Do you have more?" she asked the girl.

White Dove brought the bowl and placed it at Dora's feet. Several leaves of the plant were soaking in water.

"Did you heat the water?" The girl nodded and smiled. Dora's heart melted at the smile. It would be nice to have a daughter. For a brief moment, she thought about asking the chief if he would consider letting White Dove stay with them once they found their people. She needed a mother. But she knew he would never agree. It was not the way of the Indian people. They took care of their own. She thought of the child inside her. It was close to the stage in her pregnancy when she had lost the others and she would not rest easy until that stage passed. She lifted a silent prayer. "Lord God, if you see fit to let this baby live, I'll see fit to teach her your ways so she can walk with you."

She felt somewhat guilty after the prayer as if she had been bargaining with God. But it was true. She and Rafe had taught Tom to love God and he was a good boy. She was already calling this one a girl. Maybe it was because of Alice.

She shifted her focus to the job at hand. "You've done well," she said to the girl and finished removing the poultice. "The stench is gone. That means it's healing. I'll add some of these mint leaves to help with the pain." She cleaned the wound with a cloth dipped in the hot kettle, put another poultice on it and reban-daged it.

"You rest this morning," she told the chief. "My man will come by later to help you stand and walk. We've decided to leave tonight. You and the girl will go with us. The soldiers have headed east, and we'll be going west so we shouldn't run into any trouble."

Rafe expected the same firmness from the old man that he had displayed the day before and was surprised when he looked into

Dora's eyes and nodded. "I will live. We go with you." He looked at Rafe. "Your woman is right. Best leave at night."

Rafe had hoped that they would be on their way this morning, but who was he to argue with an Indian Chief and a wife too big for her britches.

THE CHIEF WAS MORE agile than Rafe had thought. His muscles were weak in the injured leg from not moving it, but while he was so badly wounded, he'd had the presence of mind to keep his other limbs moving so they would not weaken. He had donned his sash and was looking quite fierce and regal. Rafe could well imagine what he had been like in his younger years. Rafe and Tom helped him climb down from the rock. By the end of the day, he was walking with the aid of a makeshift crutch Tom had carved from a slender dogwood tree.

It was almost nightfall. The sky was a glorious orange color to the west and Dora remarked that it was a good sign. The setting sun was urging them to move on. Dora made room in the back on the wagon for the old man and as they helped him climb in, Rafe sent Tom and the girl to the creek with buckets to fill up the water barrel.

Tom and White Dove had learned to communicate with few words and seemed to know what the other was thinking. The girl laughed when they bent at the exact same time to dip the buckets in the water, bumping their heads, and they both exaggerated the heaviness of the buckets when they sat them down. But before Tom could pick his bucket back up, someone grabbed him from behind and the girl screamed.

"Oginalii!" she cried. It was the word for brother. She started hitting at the dark-skinned arm that was holding Tom captive. There was a knife in his hand, and she tried to knock it away.

"E-lu-we-i," he said, putting his other hand over her mouth trying to hush her. She broke away and ran toward the wagon screaming for help.

Rafe heard her cries and grabbed his gun from the back of the wagon and started running her way.

"Help me down," the chief insisted. Dora helped him climb down and reached for Tom's old Winchester. By this time, the girl had reached the wagon and pulled on her grandfather's arm.

"Ashkii," she shouted. "Ashkii here. He has Tom." Dora was surprised at the girl's sudden ability to speak their language. Had she been holding back? And who was Ashkii, and what was he doing with her boy?

She lifted the rifle and walked boldly to the woods where Rafe had disappeared.

"Wait," the old man shouted. "Ashkii is girl's brother."

"I don't care if he's a leprechaun," she said, going full steam ahead. "He'd better not hurt my boy!"

Just then, Rafe and the others rounded the bend. Rafe had a firm hold on the young man and the knife was nowhere to be seen. Tom scooted on ahead.

"Ashkii," the chief said firmly. "Oganalii—friend." He waved his arms to encompass the McCades. "These are our friends."

The young man looked deflated and embarrassed. He'd had a chance to prove his bravery and his own sister had spoiled it. He looked at her and scowled and then spoke in English to his grandfather. "The others come soon, Enisi. They sent me ahead."

"Give me your arm, Ashkii," the chief said. "We go out to meet them."

The young man held on to his grandfather's arm, but before they could take any steps, the sound of hoofbeats filled the air and suddenly they were surrounded by a dozen Indians, some with their arrows drawn tight in their bows. Dora was still holding her rifle and she raised it.

The chief bellowed out a command and held his arms out. The young warriors relaxed, and Dora lowered her rifle. It had been a tense moment.

"We meet in council," the chief said, pulling the men aside. After a few moments, his grandson helped him walk back to the wagon.

The chief spoke to Dora. "We go with them. The Ponca tribe to the north will give us shelter and we will stay with them until we can get back to our on people." He took the ornate necklace from around his neck and handed it to Dora. "Your medicine is good. You keep this."

She was touched. "Thank you," she said as he dropped it into her hand. "I will wear it and think of you and White Dove." She pulled the girl to her in a hug. "Take good care of your grandfather." The girl smiled and walked away.

One of the warriors helped the old chief upon a horse, then sat the girl on the horse with her brother. They turned their horses north. "Go in peace," Rafe called out to them. The girl turned back and waved.

Dora watched their horses canter off and stood with the necklace in her hand. She held it up and studied it. "It's nice, isn't it?" she asked Rafe.

"That's got some value to it. Maybe you shouldn't have taken it.".

"You don't understand Indian ways. He thinks I saved his life and woulda thought I was turning up my nose at his gift if I had refused it. He felt beholdin' to me."

Rafe grinned. "In that case, I wish he had felt beholdin' enough to give you that fancy sash he was wearing. I kinda liked it."

She stuck out her tongue and made a face at him. "You're an old snake, Rafe McCade." She flicked her skirt and walked away. "Since the horses are hitched up, let's get out of here."

"You sure you don't want to spend another night? Since the old man and girl have gone, we don't need to sneak out of here in the dark."

"No," she said. He thought he saw a tear roll down her cheek before she turned away. "Let's move on if you've still a mind to it. It'll be too lonesome here with the girl gone."

CHAPTER EIGHT
BAD BISCUITS

They were in Indian Territory, soon to be called Kansas. They were several days out of Independence, and the sea of prairie grass looked as if it would never end. Cotton Bailey and his wife, Jenny, had joined them in Independence and Dora was glad of it. The monotonous scenery would have driven her crazy if not for Jenny. She had the voice of an angel but the personality of a mischievous child. And she wasn't much more than a child. She was just sixteen—barely three years older than Tom. She was paper-thin and had long blonde hair. And Tom was fairly smitten with her. Dora had noticed and wanted to put a stop to it, but Cotton just laughed. "Leave him alone," he said. "He's just never seen a pretty girl before. I remember being that age and it wasn't that many years ago."

Cotton's name was Alfred, but his nickname suited him well. He was a young man—not yet twenty, but his hair and eyelashes were as white as an old man's, and his eyes were a pale blue with a hint of pink on the outer iris. During the day, he wore long sleeves and a hat pulled down over his eyes to keep his skin from burning. Rafe said his lack of color was due to being albino, but

Dora had never seen a man so white. She'd seen a white deer once, so she reckoned it was the same thing.

Earlier that day, they met a small group of soldiers from Fort Union who were on their way southeast to check out some Indian trouble they'd gotten wind of. Rafe rode out to meet them. The commanding officer halted his men and he and Rafe dismounted and talked for a while.

"Where are you folks headed?" he asked Rafe.

"We're headed first to Willow Bar. From there we'll be leaving the trail and going northwest to a place called Big Sandy. Have you heard of it?"

"I passed through in November—met some nice folks on a ranch in the valley there. They put me and my men up in their barn for a few days when we got caught in an early winter storm. Name was McCade. He and the missus had a young boy and a new baby. There's plenty of room along the Big Sandy if a fellow has a mind to settle there. If you happen to meet McCade, let him know I'll be back to visit someday."

Rafe grinned. It was a big country but not so full of people as to be too unusual for the major to have run across Colin. "So, Colin McCade's a new daddy? Boy or girl?"

The major looked at him with interest. "A boy. How do you know McCade?"

"He's my brother. That's where we're headed. I'm Rafe McCade."

The officer held out his hand to shake. "Well, I'll be! I'm Major Frank Adams. Pretty country up there. You shouldn't have any Indian trouble."

"That's good to know. What about between here and there? Will we likely run into any Indians?"

"You're bound to run into some. This whole area is set aside for Indian Territory, but that's changing. Some settlers have been illegally squatting on the land and that's caused trouble—some uprisings. We've been sent to settle things down if we can."

Rafe nodded. "We came across two cabins built side-by-side near a creekbank two days back. We stopped to fill up our water barrels. I didn't know they were squatters. They seemed nice enough."

"Sodbusters, they call 'em. Most of the folks are fine people. They're tired, they see a place to light and they decide they don't want to go any farther west. I can't blame them. As long as they have access to water during the dry spells, they'll grow some crops here. It's not the best soil in the world, but it'll do. I figure in another year the government will move the Indians south of here and open this land up for settlement." He paused. "But as for your question about trouble, I don't see the Indians causing you any as long as they know you're just passing through."

"And if they do give us trouble?" Rafe asked.

The major assessed the two families.

"You have anyone else in your wagon?"

"No, just the five of us."

"Then you wouldn't have much of a chance."

Rafe grinned. "We might be little, but we've got some fight in us. You haven't seen my boy and my wife handle a gun." He pointed to the couple in the back wagon. "And those two are too young and full of themselves to be afraid. I hope we don't have to deal with trouble, but we'll do what we gotta do if faced with a battle."

The major smiled. "I like your style, McCade." He pointed to Rafe's holster. "I see you've got a sidearm too. You're liable to need it before you get to New Mexico Territory."

"So I was told. I already had the pistol, but I bought the holster back in Independence. Figured I might need it."

"Every man wears one west of here. It can be good and bad. Hard drinking and hot tempers don't mix well, and some can be too quick to use a gun."

"I'll remember that."

"If you have any trouble between here and there, Fort Atkinson is less than a mile from where you'll be crossing the river. Tell them I sent you, and they'll provide whatever you need. You'll likely see some Indian encampments outside the fort. The fort is understaffed, but there's a good Indian agent that keeps them in line."

"Thank you, sir. I appreciate your time."

Major Adams mounted his horse and Rafe did the same.

"There is one thing to watch out for though," the major said. "A small band of Pawnees have been pestering the wagons traveling through, but they haven't hurt anyone as far as I know. They're beggars and they'll be trying to get you to feed them. My advice to you is, don't do it. Once you do, they'll try to scare you into keeping on feeding them and they'll follow you until you run out of food."

"Why would they be hungry? We haven't had any trouble finding rabbits and quail."

"They're not hungry. There's plenty of meat to eat, but they've taken a special liking to biscuits and flapjacks."

"They have flour and cornmeal, don't they? Why don't they make their own bread?"

"This band doesn't have any squaws with them, but that's not the reason they beg for biscuits. The Indians don't have any leavening powder and once they've had the taste of a white woman's biscuits or flapjacks, they acquire a taste for it."

"If they ever tasted my woman's biscuits, they'd probably steal her away from me," Rafe said, laughing.

"They might at that. You're making me hungry. I haven't had a good biscuit since we camped at your brother's place."

"You're welcome to stay and eat with us. We'll be stoppin' to make camp in a couple of hours; sooner if your men will eat with us. We'll scare up some rabbits and have a feast."

"That's awfully tempting, but we've got to be moving on. Oh, another thing: if you run across those Indians, they'll pretend they don't understand our language, but they do. They've had plenty of practice."

Rafe thanked him for his advice and the soldiers went on their way. He went back to the wagon to tell Cotton what the major had said.

"We'll stop for the night in a couple of hours, Cotton. We've been going since dawn and the horses are tired. I doubt we'll run into any Indians today, but we'll keep a watch during the night."

An hour later, Tom hollered from the wagon. "Pa, there's some horses up ahead. Looks like Indians to me."

Rafe had lulled himself into a trance with nothing but tall grass to look at, and he was thankful for Tom's sharp eyes.

"It is Indians," he said, and pulled back to the wagon. "Just keep a steady pace and don't show any fear. I'll drop back and let Cotton know."

He gave the Baileys the same advice. "They'll probably be begging for food. Let on like you don't have any."

"First time I've seen Indians," Cotton said. He didn't sound afraid; just curious. He grinned at his wife. "If they were to eat Jenny's biscuits, they wouldn't be begging for any food from us."

Jenny scowled at him. Well, you've been eating 'em, Cotton Bailey, and I haven't heard any complaints."

"No need to—they've kept me alive, ain't they? He moved his head to the left to avoid the hand that was getting ready to flatten his hat. "And that's all I'm gonna say about that."

Rafe laughed. "That gives me an idea. Just keep it steady. If we stop our wagon, you stop too. Have your gun ready just in case." Rafe rode back up to his own wagon, jumped on the buckboard, and tied his horse to the lead rope. Tom handed him the reins and slipped inside the wagon. He handed his ma the shotgun, but he stayed in the back with his Winchester.

It was a ragtag group of eight braves, and they had no guns among them—only bows and arrows. There didn't appear to be a chief; if there was, he didn't wear any special adornment. There were two young braves, but the others were middle-aged or older. The group rode tight together until they got close to the McCade wagon. One of them broke away and moved forward. He had a few teeth missing and seemed to be the leader. He held his hand out motioning for the wagon to stop and when Rafe didn't, he looked surprised and moved out of the way. He lined himself up with the horses and rode along beside them. The other Indians looked at each other in confusion and watched their leader for direction. When none was forthcoming, they waited where they were.

"You're awful brave," Dora said quietly. "There are eight of them and four of us."

"Five," Tom corrected her from behind the curtain.

"I wasn't leaving you out, boy. Jenny doesn't have a gun."

"That doesn't matter," Tom said. "She'd jump on 'em with her bare hands."

Dora chuckled. "That she would." She looked at Rafe. "Aren't you scared they'll try to shoot us with their arrows?"

"They're smarter than that, Dora. They know we have guns and by the time they get their arrows loaded, we could shoot most of them."

"But what if there's more hiding somewhere?"

"I don't think that's likely. This is the band Major Adams was telling me about. We'll stop in a few minutes to make camp and when we do, I want you to make biscuits bad enough that a dog wouldn't eat them." He turned to her and smiled. "You think you can do that?"

"I'll make 'em. They haven't been much good anyway since we sold Daisy back in Independence. You need milk to make good biscuits."

"You'll need to make them a lot worse than that—dry and taste-less and maybe burn them a little bit. We'll all eat them, and we'll pretend they're the best biscuits we've ever had."

The Indian dropped back so he was riding even with Rafe. He rubbed his stomach and made a pained expression.

"Are you sick?" Rafe asked him.

The Indian shook his head. "Hungry," he answered.

"We don't have any food. We'll make camp soon. My woman will make biscuits."

The man smiled showing an almost toothless grin. "Biscuits good."

"We don't have any meat," Rafe said. "We were hoping to kill some rabbits."

"We have rabbits. Your woman make biscuits?"

"Yes, if you share your rabbits."

The Indian nodded and rode back to his group. He conferred with them and they all whooped and laughed and rode with the wagon at a distance until they stopped thirty minutes later and made camp.

"I hate wastin' good flour like this," Dora told Jenny as she started bringing out the ingredients.

"You can use mine," Jenny said. "Cotton don't like my biscuits anyway. Hold on—I'll be right back." She ran to the back of their wagon and brought out the sack of flour. It was almost empty but had enough to make what they needed.

"You shouldn't keep it out in the open, Jenny. It'll go bad. You should always keep your flour in a wood barrel." She opened it up and measured it out in the bowl. She got a whiff of the smell and turned up her nose.

"No wonder he don't like your biscuits," Dora said. "This flour's gone rancid."

Jenny sighed. "So we'll have to use yours then?"

"No, not at all," Dora said with a gleam in her eye. "Rafe told me to make bad tastin' biscuits so the Indians wouldn't follow us. This will do it. The worst thing is, we're supposed to pretend like they're good. I'm not sure I can stomach a rancid biscuit."

"We've been doin' it," Jenny said, laughing.

"If I'd known that, I woulda give you some of my flour."

"It's good you didn't 'cause I would have thrown mine out and you wouldn't be making bad biscuits with it right now."

"You're beginning to think like me, Jenny girl. Let's get cooking. Why don't you skedaddle over there and make sure Rafe's got coals hot enough for the oven. We'll fix up a big batch and those Indians will think they've struck gold."

"Until they bite into them," Jenny said, and they both laughed.

THE RABBITS CAME off the spit at the same time the biscuits came out of the oven. The braves looked at the huge platter with appreciation. The man with few teeth reached for one, but Rafe pushed the platter back and proceeded to cut up the rabbits. When he reached again, Dora moved the platter out of the way.

"We must ask the Lord to bless this food before we eat," she said, wagging her finger at the Indian. "Rafe, would you say our blessing?"

They bowed their heads and the braves watched curiously as Rafe prayed. "Lord, we thank you for our friends who are sharing our table. We pray that our meager fare nourishes and fills our stomachs. Bless the meat they provided, and when they eat, hurry them along on their way. In Jesus name we pray. Amen."

"Amen," the others repeated. Even the Indians said a few amens. Rafe felt a little guilty as he dug into the rabbit that Dora served upon his plate. He then took a bite of his biscuit. It was the worst thing he'd ever put in his mouth, but he chewed on it and smiled. The others followed suit and pretty soon they were all eating and talking. Except for the Indians. One by one, they took bites of the biscuits and tried to chew them. They looked around at each other, then looked at Rafe and then at Dora.

"Uh, oh," Dora said under her breath. "Maybe this wasn't such a good idea."

"Just keep chewing and pretend it's good," Rafe said.

One of the young men spit his bite into the fire and threw the rest of the biscuit in with it. He got up and grabbed the three remaining rabbits and walked to his horse. The others followed him, but the lead Indian stayed behind.

"Are you leaving so soon," Rafe asked, looking confused. "Wait and I'll pack some of the biscuits for you to take with you."

"No," the Indian said, holding out his hand to protest. "We take rabbits." He looked at Dora, shook his head, and then looked back at Rafe. "Why you keep woman?" he asked. "She make bad biscuits." And with that, he followed the others and they rode away.

"What are we going to eat?" Tom asked, standing up and throwing his biscuit in the fire. "I didn't get a bite of rabbit and that Indian's right—those are bad biscuits."

Everyone else broke out in laughter. Tom opened his mouth and looked at them suspiciously. "Well, they are bad," he said. "And you're all eating them like they're good."

Jenny smiled. "They are good for something, Tom," she said. "They're good for keeping the Indians away."

Dora watched as Tom's anger melted at the sound of Jenny's voice and he quieted down. She punched Rafe with her elbow. "Look at that," she said. "Our boy's growing up."

"Poor Tom," he said. "One smile from a woman and he's done for."

Tom came out of his trance-like state and jumped up. "Well, what are we going to eat? I'm starving."

Rafe turned to Dora. "There's still hope as long as his stomach rules instead of his heart."

She laughed and pulled a plate from under the tablecloth. "I made a good batch of biscuits while I was making the bad."

Rafe spoke up. "And I put one rabbit aside while I was cutting them up. That rabbit's going to be stretched five ways, but we'll make do. Those nine Indians are feasting on rabbits, but they won't be bothering us anymore."

They went to bed with full stomachs and light laughter still in their hearts.

CHAPTER NINE
DEVIL WIND

The terrain gradually changed, and Dora was glad of it. Gently rolling hills were on the horizon. Here they found shorter grass and small groupings of trees scattered across the landscape. The trail had followed a small stream for miles, but it did nothing to cool off the intense August heat. Just that morning, they came upon a group of cowhands driving a herd from Texas to Abilene. The drover told them that they were just a day's ride from Fort Atkinson. This was welcome news to Rafe. Colin's crude map showed the fort to be just a short distance from the ford where they planned to cross the Arkansas river. They would be there tomorrow, and he could mark off one more milestone of their journey.

"Be careful," the drover said. "The heat and humidity today is liable to cause some storms this afternoon. When Jake over there gets skittish and looks off in the distance, we know to be wary."

"What makes him think there'll be a storm?" Rafe asked.

"Apaches killed Jake's pa and kidnapped Jake when he was twelve-years-old. An army patrol rescued him about two years later, but he's still got some of the Indian ways about him. Indians in this part of the country have seen a lot of storms, and they have a good sense about when one's coming. They can feel it in the air. Jake learned a right smart from the Indians. He's good to have around."

"Thank you for the warning. We've been in a few big storms— lots of thunder and bad lightning just two days back. It came up real sudden-like and I was wishing we had more shelter to hole up in. The wagons seem mighty flimsy in a storm."

"This is worse than a storm. They're called tornadoes but Jake calls them devil winds. He says he's seen one pluck trees right out of the ground and drop them half a mile away. It'll carry your wagon plum off if you're caught up in it."

"I've never been in one of those storms but I've heard tell of them. I hope Jake's wrong."

"I hope so too. I can't afford to lose any cows."

"What should I watch for?"

"You'll see a cloud that looks like a spinning top. It comes right down and picks up everything in its path. If it gets close enough, you'll see things flying in the air. Stay away from trees, and don't let the horses panic; you'll need them calm to get out of its path."

"I don't like the sound of that. I'll tell the others."

Rafe was watchful for the rest of the morning. "Keep your eye on the sky," he told Cotton. "Front and back, and if you see any black clouds that look like they're dropping from the sky, take off in another direction. It could be a tornado."

"I've always wanted to see one," Cotton said with a grin.

"I don't care to see one at all," Rafe said. "The drover said it could pick a wagon straight up off the ground—horses and all—and set 'em down a half-mile away."

"We're going to stop and water the horses," Cotton said. "We've come a far piece this morning and they need the rest. With only the two of 'em, they have to work harder than yours. You go on ahead. We'll catch up."

It was true. The McCades had lost some time because of the Baileys' having to rest their horses so often, but they were good company to ride with. Rafe turned his horse back to the wagon; he was anxious to move on. He climbed onto the buckboard and hurried the horses along. "Thank goodness," Dora said when he sat down beside her. "My arms are about worn out. We should rest here for a while."

"You can rest in the back of the wagon," he told her. "Keep a watch on the sky from the back and send Tom up here to ride with me."

"Storm a'brewing?" she asked.

He nodded. "Could be a bad one. I don't know which direction it'll come from if it does."

"I ain't heard a peep out of him, so he must be asleep. I'll wake him up."

"Not much else to do when we're riding like this."

"He needs to be walking along with the wagon now and then or he's gonna get lazy. I'm getting hungry; are you?"

"I could use a bite. You got any biscuits left from breakfast?"

"Don't I always?" she said and laughed. "Those poor Indians. They'd still be following us if they'd tasted my real biscuits."

"That they would, woman—that they would! Have Tom bring me a couple. And maybe some jerky."

Rafe kept the horses at a steady pace south with Tom riding beside him. Dark clouds were rolling in but nothing yet to alarm him. "Look behind us, boy and see if Cotton has caught up with us yet."

Tom stretched his body to the left and looked back. "I can't see him from this side, Pa. I'll get in the back of the wagon and look." He pushed his way into the back and called out. "Ma's asleep. She must be tuckered out." It didn't take but a few seconds until he poked his head through the front canvas.

"It's real dark back there, Pa. I think I see Cotton's wagon, but it's a whole lot worse behind us than it is ahead. It's real dusty and there's some big old clouds sittin' almost on the ground."

Rafe started turning the horses so he could see. "Wake your Ma up. I'm turning around." He circled to the right and was alarmed at what he saw. Off in the distance, just as Tom said, the clouds looked as if they were touching the ground. It was like a long arm reaching out of the sky and it was headed toward Cotton's wagon. He wondered if they even saw it, but they had to have heard it. He was just beginning to hear the roar of it.

Dora stuck her head through the opening. "Lord have mercy, Rafe. I fell asleep and didn't see it coming."

"Get the gun and fire a warning shot up into the air. I hope and pray Cotton and Jenny have seen it and are trying to get away. It snuck up behind us. Can you tell which way it's going?"

"It's coming this way." She pointed to the left. "Go thataway, hurry!"

Rafe tapped the horse ahead of him lightly with the whip. "Git," he said. The horses, fearing the change in the weather, did as they were told and raced off to the left.

"Lord in heaven," Dora shouted to the sky. "Be with those kids and keep them safe from harm's way. Lord, if I'd been watchin' like I was supposed to, we could'a warned them. Don't take my mistake out on them two youngin's. I ask you in the name of Jesus, Amen."

Big tears were mixed in with the raindrops that were falling down her face. "Rafe, I'll never forgive myself if something happens to them."

"Dora, it wouldn't be your fault. I told them to watch the sky front and back. I just wish they'd kept up with us." Rafe was a lot more worried than he was letting on to Dora. He'd grown to like the young couple a lot and couldn't stand to think something might happen to them.

The rain came down hard and the wind was strong, but they continued heading as fast as they could away from the path of the tornado. "Keep watching, Dora. I've heard tell of these things making twists and turns. They don't always go straight ahead."

She stepped back through the opening to look out the back. Tom was huddled in the corner.

"Is it over, Ma?" He was trembling. "I was watching from the back but when the wind got up, I was scared."

"There's nothing wrong with being scared, son. Me and your Pa are scared too. I'll check on things back here," she said, making her way to the back opening. She stayed back there watching for a short while, then headed to the front.

"Rafe, I've never seen the likes! It went through that patch of trees like they were matchsticks. It snapped them off in mid-air. But it's heading southeast now so I don't think we're in danger." She wrung her hands. "I'm sure worried about those youngin's, though. Let's hurry back and check on 'em."

Rafe stopped the horses and stepped down from the wagon. He walked to the back and looked in the direction they had just come from. It didn't look good. He slowly shuffled his way to the front of the wagon and started to mount his horse. "Dora, you and Tom stay here with the wagon. I'll take the horse and go back."

"You're not looking me in the eye, Rafe McCade," she said. "You're worried about what you'll find, aren't you?"

He sighed and looked up. "If it was snapping off trees, there's no telling what it did to their wagon. I don't want you and Tom to see it."

"You're not going without me. They might be hurt, and I can do something to help 'em."

Rafe knew there was no use arguing with her, so he climbed in the wagon again, turned the horses and headed back. The sky was still dark, but the twister was no longer in sight. It had disappeared back up into the air. Dora was right. The line of trees up on the hill had a swath cut out right in the middle of it. As they passed by, it looked as if the trees had been twisted off their trunks and they were laying topsy-turvy everywhere they looked.

As the sky lightened, they could make out the form of the wagon, but as they got closer, they could see it was turned over on its side. The horses were scattered a hundred yards away from the wagon but didn't seem to be in distress. They were calmly munching on grass.

"They must be in the wagon," Dora said when they didn't see any sign of Cotton and Jenny. "Hurry Rafe!"

The contents of the wagon were strewn everywhere. Dora searched inside while Rafe searched underneath the upended wagon. They were nowhere to be seen.

"You don't think they got blown away, do you, Pa?" Tom asked.

"I don't know what to think, boy," Rafe answered. "The way it tore up those trees, it could have easily picked up a man."

Tom had tears in his eyes. "Or a woman," he said.

"Let's don't get ahead of ourselves. We'll spread out and look through the grass. It's tall enough in some places to hide those two as thin as they are." But he was worried. The drover said that a tornado could lift a whole wagon and drop it down a far piece away. If those kids had been picked up by the wind, they wouldn't have survived it.

Dora was already moving toward the trees. "Rafe, look!" she said pointing ahead. "There's a small ravine just beyond this hill. Maybe they rode the storm out there."

Rafe and Tom broke out in a run and they all topped the hill at about the same time. What they saw filled them all with dread.

Dora swiftly went into action. "Tom, get my medicine bag from the wagon and there's an old sheet in grandpa's trunk that we can cut in strips. Bring a bucket of water too, and my dishpan."

"I don't think I can carry it all in one trip," Tom said.

"Use my horse," Rafe said. "Get back here as fast as you can."

"Yes, sir," he said, and started running.

Cotton was pinned under a large limb that had blown from a tree over fifty yards away. His head was covered with blood and his right leg was at an odd angle. Jenny was nowhere to be seen.

"Help me lift this limb, Dora, but whatever you do, don't let it drop back on him. Lift and shove at the same time."

"Is he alive?" she asked.

"We won't know until we get this off of him. There are too many branches in the way. I'm going to get here in the center, and you lift from that end."

She thought about the baby and what damage might be done by lifting such a load. "It's heavy, Rafe. Let's wait until Tom gets back. He can pull him out from under it if we can lift it high enough."

"Okay, we'll wait, but the sooner we get it off, the better."

She looked back at the wagon. "There he comes now."

He looked around. "I wonder where Jenny is?"

"We'll take one thing at a time," she said, looking worried. "Here's Tom with the horse."

"Let me lift, and you pull him out, Ma. I'm afraid I'll hurt him."

Under normal conditions, Dora would have argued. She prided herself for being strong for her size, but now she just felt relief. Cotton was a small man and she wouldn't have any trouble at all pulling him out. God had provided a solution and she was glad of it.

Tom and Rafe lifted together at the count of three and were able to hold up long enough for Dora to pull Cotton out from under the limb.

"He's alive," she said, and knelt down beside him. "Now you two get to looking for Jenny-girl and I'll work on this one."

She was glad to see the head wound was not as serious as she first thought. He was unconscious, but as she ran her fingers through his hair, she determined there were no indentions in his skull. A concussion was possible but unlikely. The limbs of the tree had cut up his face and scalp. She knew that even minor cuts on the scalp can bleed heavily so she wasn't so worried about that. The leg was another matter. It was broken and if they didn't get it set and splinted soon, it would cause problems later. It was a blessing that he was knocked out because pulling a bone back into place was a painful thing.

She poured water into the dishpan and went about cleaning up his head making sure to get all the bits and pieces of bark and leaves out of the wounds. It would have helped to have hot water but there was no time to build a fire and heat it.

His heartbeat was steady but slow. She carefully felt from his ribcage down to his abdomen to see if there were internal injuries. She didn't feel anything abnormal, but it was impossible to tell right away. Rafe would need to help her set the leg by pulling the bone in place. She tore more strips from the sheet. There were some sturdy branches on the tree that would make good splints. She'd send Tom to the wagon for the ax.

She finished checking him over and looked up. Where were Tom and Rafe? Had they found Jenny?

After a few minutes, she heard voices and stood up. Rafe was walking up the hill carrying Jenny in his arms.

"Thank God you found her! Is she okay?" Dora asked as he carefully laid her on the ground.

"She doesn't seem to be hurt up—it's more like she's shook up. She's shivering all over and she won't say anything. I found her huddled in the ravine down below. It was a good place to be."

"I'd be shook up too if I'd been in the middle of that tornado. I'll check her out next, but first, I need you to help me set Cotton's leg."

She turned to Tom who was sitting next to Jenny. "Tom, go up and get the ax. We'll need to trim some of these branches to make a splint."

Tom did as he was told and was back in a few minutes chopping away at the branches. They soon had the bone pulled back in place and straightened with the help of a branch on each side tied together with strips of the sheet.

Cotton began to stir, and he moaned with pain. "You're okay, boy," Rafe said, bending over him. "Dora's got you all fixed up and you'll be good as new in no time at all."

"Jenny," he moaned. "Where's Jenny?"

At the sound of Cotton's voice calling her name, Jenny came out of her trance-like state.

"Cotton! Where are you, Cotton?" she yelled, with a panic-filled expression on her face.

Dora jumped up and ran over to her, helping her stand up. "He's here, Jenny. Come with me; he's right over here."

Jenny sat cross-legged beside him and started crying uncontrollably. "He's dead, isn't he?" she cried.

"No, child. He's hurt bad, but he'll be okay." Dora hoped her words were true. They wouldn't know until he came to, and maybe not even then if he was hurt inside. Those kinds of injuries sometimes don't show up for a day or two.

Jenny stopped crying, calmed by Dora's words. "We were stopped when we saw it coming. Cotton said we wouldn't have time to run the wagon away from it, so he pushed me forward and told me to head for that ditch and he would be right behind me after he unhooked the horses. Me and those horses were all he was thinking about." She started crying again, softly this time. "The last thing I saw before I hit the ditch was trees whirling up into the air. I don't remember anything after that."

Rafe sat down beside her. "You're both lucky to be alive is all I can say." He looked over at the wagon. "He was wise to turn the horses loose. If they'd been hooked to the wagon when it turned over, they would have gone down with it and more than likely had some broken bones."

"But it almost cost him his own life," Dora said. "Men! I wonder sometimes if any of you have a lick of sense. Jenny could do without those horses a heap more than she could do without her man."

"I guess we do have a quare way of lookin' at things, don't we? I reckon that's just our nature." He grinned. "But we're lucky to have you women to set us in our place now and again."

"What will happen to our wagon?" Jenny asked. "Will we have to leave it here?"

"Nah. It's a little worse for wear, but with the help of the horses, I think we can get it upright. Most everything in it got wet but we'll see what we can save." Rafe gave her arm a gentle squeeze and stood up. "We'll stay here tonight. We all need to rest."

He nodded to Tom who had remained quiet the whole time. "Let's get to work, boy. We'll need to get Cotton up off this wet ground and the best place for him is in the back of his wagon. We can't do that with it turned on its side."

After they left, Dora started examining Jenny. "You don't seem hurt at all, Jenny-girl. Your man knew what he was doing sending you into that ditch. You're soaking wet through and through, but your clothes will dry quick-like in this blazing sun." She stood up. "Which reminds me, we need to get some shade on Cotton's face. How about breaking a branch from the limb here —one that's still got leaves on it and hold it over him so he won't burn."

Jenny jumped to her feet, anxious for something to do. "It don't take much for his face to get burnt, with him being so pale. When I met him, I knew he was the one the good Lord sent to rescue me from my daddy. I had dreams at night about someone good coming to get me out of the mess I was in, and it was always someone with a white glow about him."

She broke a branch from the tree and sat near Cotton's head. The leaves from the branch shielded his face from the brutal heat. Dora let her continue with her story, knowing it would be good for her to talk instead of just worrying about her man.

"My momma died when I was just shy of ten years old and I know it was from the hands of my daddy. He was a mean one and had a bad temper about him. She wore his bruises day in and day out, and it was mostly 'cause of her getting in the middle of him knocking my older brothers around."

Dora had known men back in the hills who thought nothing of beating their wives. It made her burnin' mad just thinking about a big old man hitting a defenseless woman.

"Why didn't your ma take you kids and run off?" she asked.

"There was nowhere to run. People in them parts are dirt poor. They can't afford to take care of their own families, much less take on another woman and her youngins. Besides, people were afraid of Pa."

"I know what it's like to be poor," Dora said. "But there ain't no excuse for bein' mean because of it. What happened to your ma, child?"

"Me and my brothers were workin' in the field one day and Pa came out of the house and told us Ma was dead. He said she died of a diseased heart. It was diseased alright—broke right in two from the way he treated her. I ran back inside and there she lay with blood coming out of her mouth and nose. She'd hit her head on the table when he knocked her down. Clyde, that's my oldest brother, he went into a rage and accused Pa of killing her. He knocked Pa out cold and he landed on the floor in a big heap. If Clyde hadn't run away, I know Pa would have killed him too. We buried her on the hill next to the garden spot and after that I tried to keep my distance from Pa, but he'd catch ahold of me and slap me if I burned the bread or didn't do my chores right."

Dora sighed. "Shouldn't nobody have to live like that, Jenny-girl. I'm sorry you did."

Jenny smiled. "But I didn't have to live that way forever. Like I said, I kept dreaming about a man riding in a wagon, white from head to foot. So, when Cotton's wagon stopped at our cabin one day to water his horses, I knew he was the one."

"What did Cotton think about that?" Dora asked.

"I was lucky that Pa had gone into town that day. I couldn't take my eyes off Cotton and he noticed it right away. I pumped water in the trough for his horses and he asked me what happened to my face. I had a big bruise on it. I pulled up my sleeve and showed him my arm and told him that my Pa had done it."

Jenny sat up straight and a sweet smile started at her mouth and went all the way to her eyes. "I told him I'd been dreaming about him rescuing me and he smiled and said he'd been dreaming about a girl in a cornflower blue dress." She paused. "And that's exactly what I had on that day—a cornflower blue dress! See, Dora, it was meant to be."

Dora wasn't a bit ashamed of the tears coming from her eyes. She hugged the girl and said, "It sure was meant to be, Jenny-girl."

"Cotton told me to go pack my clothes and I could go with him. I didn't waste any time cause I didn't know when Pa and Otis would be back. I wrote a note and told them I had gone to a neighbor's house and would be back in time to cook supper. I knew that would give us a headstart before he came lookin' for me. I sure would'a liked to seen his face when he figured out I wasn't coming back."

"Did he try to find you?"

"I don't know. Cotton was good about coverin' up tracks and we rode nigh on two days and nights without hardly stopping. After a few days, we found a preacher and he married us." She smiled and brushed Cotton's hair back from his face. "Then we came on out here. I know that God sent him to me, Dora. That's why he put the dream in my head." She bent down and kissed her husband lightly on his bandaged cheek.

"He is going to be alright, ain't he?" she asked.

"He'll be fine. We'll rush on to Fort Atkinson. There'll be a doctor there. He'll have to stay until he can ride again and then you can be on your way."

"I sure am grateful to you. We're just a couple of kids and we never would have made it this far without you and Rafe."

"You've been good company, Jenny. I almost feel like you're my own little girl. We'll miss you when we leave you at the fort."

"And you've been like the mama I lost too early. She would thank you too for taking such good care of me."

They both heard the moan at the same time. "He's waking up," Jenny said. "Cotton, are you alright?"

"Ohh, it hurts. My leg hurts." He opened his eyes and looked around, then focused on Jenny. "What happened?"

"Oh Cotton! I'm so glad you're awake. I've been so worried about you. You got knocked over by a tree durin' the storm. Dora fixed you up and you're gonna be alright."

He tried to sit up but groaned again when he saw that he couldn't move his leg. "How bad am I hurt," he asked Dora. "What's wrong with my leg?"

"It was a clean break, Cotton. Me and Rafe pulled it back into place and put splints on it. It'll do until we get to Fort Atkinson and you can be seen by a doctor."

His eyes searched Jenny's. "Are you hurt, Jenny?"

"No, not a scratch on me, Cotton. You saved my life by pushing me to that ditch." She grinned. "You rescued me again."

He tried to sit up again, and this time Dora held onto his arm and pulled him up so he could lean against Jenny. "The horses? Are they alive?"

Dora nodded. "Rafe said you did a smart thing turning them loose like that. The wagon turned over, but he thinks he can right it by using the horses. That's what he and the boy are doing now."

"I wish I could help them."

"They won't have any trouble. Rafe knows about doing things like that." Her heart swelled with pride. It was true; her man knew how to do most anything. He had a good head on his shoulders. He was her man in white, just like Cotton was to Jenny. He had rescued her from a life of poverty in the hill country. She'd known hunger in her childhood years, but never since she'd married Rafe. She closed her eyes for a moment and thanked the Lord for giving her a good man.

CHAPTER TEN
FORT ATKINSON

They spent the night so Cotton wouldn't have to be moved so soon after his injuries. The next morning it was decided that Tom would ride with Jenny. Cotton would ride in the back of the McCade wagon where he would be more comfortable until Rafe got them safely to Fort Atkinson so a doctor could attend to the broken leg.

Colin's map pointed to a ford about a mile south of the fort where they would cross the Arkansas river. Once they were satisfied the young couple would be taken care of, they would be on their way.

Many military posts had sprung up along the travel routes as people continued their westward migration. Federal troops were sent to protect the new settlers from Indians whose homelands were being invaded. Fort Atkinson was one such post.

As the wagons made their way to the fort, Rafe was alarmed to see large groups of Indians encamped outside the gates. Two braves mounted their horses and came to meet them.

"Get in the back of the wagon, Dora."

"Do you think the fort has been attacked?" she asked.

"I don't think so," he said. "The flag is still flying."

Just then Rafe saw the gates begin to open and two soldiers motioned them in. "Holler for Tom to pick up speed," he said. She hurried to the back of the wagon to do so. Rafe touched the flank of the horse on his left and they all broke out in a run. The Bailey's wagon followed on their heels and the two braves were left gawking.

"What are they doin' out there?" Rafe asked. "I thought the fort was being attacked."

"They were just curious," the sergeant who closed the gate said with a chuckle.

"They could easily attack if they had half a mind to," he answered. "Our numbers are low, but we can't get any reinforcements. We've only got one troop of eighty cavalrymen and there are over three-hundred Indians out there. It's been a delicate situation at times."

"What keeps them from attacking?" Rafe asked as he stepped down from the wagon.

"We've got a peace treaty right now, and we're lucky to have a good Indian Agent, Thomas Fitzpatrick. He's got a good grasp on the Indian situation and brings in regular goods for them. He's due in today with supplies. He'll bring them some pork, bread and coffee and some warm blankets for the winter. They trust Fitzpatrick, and once he dispenses the supplies, they'll be off to their winter camps. If you stay here for a day or two, you shouldn't run into them anymore."

"That's a relief. It looks like we got here at the right time." Rafe held out his hand. "I'm Rafe McCade."

The sergeant took it. "Sergeant Nathan Fields. Glad to meet you. What brings you here?"

"We ran into some trouble a day's ride back. A tornado came through and the gent I've got in the back of my wagon took a bad hit when a tree branch ran him aground. His leg is broken, and he took a few licks on the head. His name's Cotton Bailey. We were hoping to find a doctor here."

"We've got one. He's old as Methuselah, but he's as good as any I've seen." He looked at the motley group in front of him. Dora had climbed down but Tom and Jenny were still seated on the back wagon. The sergeant pointed to a small wood building. "Dr. Clarke's quarters are right there. You can pull your wagon in front of it."

"My son is driving Bailey's wagon. That's Mrs. Bailey beside him."

"She's awfully young to be a Missus," ain't she? I thought she was your daughter."

"She's older than she looks but she and her husband are both young. I figure him to be about twenty."

"We don't have much in the way of accommodations for ladies here, but the doctor's building is clean. They can wash up and make themselves comfortable."

"It's better than what we've been used to." Rafe turned around to speak to Dora. "You and Tom drive the wagons to that building over there. I'll be there in a few minutes to help you unload the boy."

The sergeant motioned to the sentry. "Private Martin, give these folks a hand. Drive this front wagon to the doctor's quarters and get someone to help get the patient out of the back." The young man did as he was told, and the wagons moved out with Dora walking behind.

"Thank you, Sergeant Fields. We met Major Frank Adams a few days back. He said if we had any trouble along the way, we could stop in here. You've been helpful."

The sergeant caught his breath. His eyes grew wide and he looked as if he'd seen a ghost. "You—you met Major Adams?"

Rafe wondered at his reaction. "Yes, he was a nice fellow—we talked for a while—he knew my brother, Colin McCade. Said he'd wintered at his ranch a few days last October."

The sergeant just stood there not saying anything.

"What's wrong? You do know Major Adams, don't you?"

The sergeant regained his composure. "I did know Major Adams —very well in fact. I rode with him on several assignments." He paused and looked down at his feet. "Mr. McCade, a rider came in early this morning with a message that Major Adams's troop was attacked by Indians and there were no survivors."

It was Rafe's turn to be shocked. The rugged major who had been so kind was dead. He'd been killed in an Indian uprising. Rafe had taken an instant liking to the major. He was the kind of man you'd be proud to ride with, but somehow the renegades had got the best of him. Rafe had been so sure they would meet again someday but now that chance was lost.

It made a man think about his own immortality. As he'd already learned, there were many hostilities facing the men and women who moved westward to settle, and now he was learning of the sacrifices made by the soldiers who tried to protect them from the Indians. They had met Indians along their journey, but none that he felt fearful of. The Cherokee had been around white men long enough to understand their ways, and they could be reasoned with. The ragtag bunch of Pawnees who had pestered them for biscuits belonged to a peaceful tribe and he had felt no danger from them. Sure, the articles and stories printed in the newspapers back home spun tales of savagery on the wild frontier, but he had assumed they were dramatized by some journalists to sell papers. His family had been lucky not to run into serious Indian trouble yet. The rest of the trip, he would be watchful and more cautious.

He realized he was standing there with his mouth open. He struggled to find words to say to the sergeant who was obviously mourning the loss of his superior officer. "He was a good man," he finally said. No other words would do.

The news of Major Adams's cavalry unit's demise at the hands of the Indians had spread amongst the troops. Adams's unit was stationed out of Fort Union but most of the old-timers at Fort Atkinson had ridden with him at one time or another. He was immensely popular among the soldiers and had gained their respect by his brave actions and his fair treatment of all who served under him. The fort was a somber place as Rafe walked to Lieutenant Henry Heth's headquarters. Lieutenant Heth was the commanding officer and had asked to speak with Rafe after finding out he had met up with Major Adams some weeks back.

Rafe talked to Lieutenant Heth for an hour. The lieutenant shared stories about Major Adams, and Rafe told him how the major warned him of the hungry Indians and how they had tricked them with bad biscuits. He told him of the tornado and how Cotton and Jenny had survived it even though they'd been right in the thick of it.

"You've been lucky in your travels thus far, Mr. McCade. I hope your luck holds out."

"I don't set much store in luck," he told the young officer. "The good Lord and a good woman have got me through thus far and that's who I'm puttin' my trust in."

Lieutenant Heth stood up and shook Rafe's hand. "You're a wise man, Rafe McCade. Give my regards to your wife and I'll lift up a prayer for your safety when you leave out tomorrow."

The lieutenant was a young but competent officer. He promised they would take good care of the Baileys until Cotton's leg healed and provide the young couple with enough food and supplies to get to Willow Bar. It made Rafe feel easier about leaving them at the fort.

THE FORT WAS nothing like Rafe had imagined. It had been hastily built the prior Fall. Sod buildings were thrown up for the troops to be quartered over the winter, but when spring arrived, they realized a permanent fort was needed. Construction materials were scarce but cottonwood and walnut trees had been hauled in from twenty-five miles south and the remainder of the fort had been built. It didn't look at all secure with big gaps without reinforcements between the sod huts in the back. Rafe wondered what would protect it from attack if the Indians rose up against the command post. The lack of trees and grass made it a cheerless place and Rafe wouldn't be sorry to leave and begin the last leg of their journey. Hearing of the major's death had trouble him and he was anxious to be gone.

The next morning, Rafe made preparations to move out. He filled their water barrels and went to purchase some supplies from the storeroom. The supply clerk was standing ready to help him.

"I'll need a slab of bacon and some sugar," he said, looking down at the list Dora had made.

"I don't have any crushed sugar, but I've got loaf sugar straight from New Orleans. I've got a stone over there you can pound it with, or you can keep it as a loaf and use nippers when you need it."

"I'd better crush it," Rafe said. "Do you have a bag I can put it in?"

"You can use a flour sack," the clerk said. "Right over there next to the bin. Don't crush it too fine, though, or it'll sift right through."

"What else is on your list?" he asked.

"Just some flour and leavening powder. I think that'll do us."

"We've got something new the missus might like to try," the clerk told him as he set the loaf of sugar on the counter. He pulled out a small tin labeled *dried milk.* "You mix it with water, and you've got milk just like it came from the cow. Our cook is tickled to death over it. He's even gone to makin' biscuits again."

"Dried milk? I wonder how they do that?" He turned the canister around and looked at the directions.

"Danged if I know. I'll put a couple of 'em in your sack."

"How much are they?"

"I'm throwing these in for free. We've got plenty to spare. We like helping out folks like you who are moving west. I'll get the bacon from the back and load all this in your wagon while you're crushing the sugar."

In just a few minutes, Rafe had the sugar crushed and walked back to the counter as the clerk came back inside.

"I've got you loaded," he said.

"Thank you. How much do I owe you?"

"Nothing. The lieutenant just now sent word while I was in the back to give you what you need, and you didn't need much."

"We're beholding to you. Give the lieutenant my regards, will you? I'll get going now so I can pick up my passengers from the doc's quarters."

"Where you headin' from here?" the clerk asked.

It seemed everyone he met asked that question and Rafe was weary of it, but he knew folks were just naturally curious. Stuck out in the middle of nowhere, they didn't get much of a chance to talk to civilians.

"We're crossing the river and heading to Willow Bar. After that, we'll be turning northwest up to Big Sandy Creek to join my brother and his family."

"That's one way of getting there," the clerk said. "Or you could cut through the Cimarron. Grass is scarce that way though and this time of year, it's hard to find water."

Rafe nodded. "My brother wrote about that route. He said we'd be better off going on to Willow Bar. Said we might have some trouble getting the wagon through some of the mountain passes after we got through the Cimarron trail."

"He's right about that, especially with a wagon. If you were on horseback, it would be the fastest way, but taking your wagon through there could be tricky. We'll be wishing you safety along the way." He reached under the counter and got a bag of peppermints. "This is for your boy." He smiled. "And for your wife. I hope you don't take offense, but I can't help noticing you got a fine lookin' missus there."

Rafe grinned. "You and everybody else. It's a good thing she don't seem to know how pretty she is, or she wouldn't pay attention to a plain looking chap like me."

He put the sugar in the back of the wagon with the rest of the supplies and hurried to the doctor's quarters. When he stepped inside, Dora and Jenny were shedding some tears saying goodbye. Rafe had copied down the directions his brother had written and handed the paper to Cotton.

"If you decide to come as far as the Big Sandy, stop in to see us. I can't speak for my brother, but if he's in need of a ranch hand, I'll put in a good word for you. He says we'll be equal partners, but I don't have much to put into his place other than a strong arm and a willingness to work. We'll be glad to have you."

"I appreciate it, Rafe. You and Dora have been good to us. We're lucky we ran into you when we did." He looked down at his leg in the cast. A rope tied to a hook in the ceiling was holding the leg at an angle, keeping it higher than his head. "Doc says I've got to keep it this way for an hour three times a day."

"You mind what that doctor tells you and you'll be up and at 'em before you know it."

He grinned. "I will. I told Jenny when we get to Willow Bar, I'll pick up a hand of dust and whichever way the wind blows it, that's the way we'll head out."

"We'll be looking for you in case it blows our way," Rafe said, and shook his hand.

CHAPTER ELEVEN
BILLY AND THE BUFFALO

They crossed the Arkansas River at the ford not far from the fort. Rafe had planned on stacking the dry goods high in the wagon, but when he saw that the water wasn't over a couple of feet deep, he decided to leave it as it was. It was an easy crossing.

The scenery changed with the miles they covered. Stubby stands of blackjack oak bordered the trail and prickly pear was in abundance. Occasionally they ran across trails made by wild horses or small groups of buffalo. Rafe shot a young elk standing no farther than fifty feet from the trail when they stopped to rest the horses under a stand of blackjack.

"I thought we'd see buffalo," Tom said when they were eating supper.

"We might when we get out in the open. Keep a watch for their dust. I've heard they sound like thunder coming from a distance."

"Or like the tornado?" Tom asked, shaking as if chilled at the memory.

"It's possible," Rafe answered, "but the ground shakes with the pounding of the buffalo hooves, especially when they're in large numbers."

"Do Indians follow the buffalo?"

Rafe hesitated and regarded his son thoughtfully. Smile lines gathered at the corner of his eyes. "You must have been talking to the soldiers?"

Tom looked at his pa and took a bite of meat. "Yeah, they said wherever you find buffalo, you'll find Injuns."

Dora scolded him. "Say yes sir to your pa, boy. And don't talk with your mouth full. You'll choke to death."

Her words were more playful than they were serious, and Tom knew it. "Yes, ma'am," he said, grinning broadly.

Rafe took a bite too and made a big display of swallowing it before he spoke. "About those buffalo..." he said, letting his sentence trail off. He looked pointedly at Dora and they all laughed.

"It's late in the year and most of them have passed through. I'm sure we'll see some buffalo—and Indians, not *Injuns*, behind them. They'll be wintering soon. The Indians will need the hides to keep them warm and the meat to keep them from going hungry. Don't worry though. They'll be so intent on the buffalo they won't pay us no mind." He hoped that was true.

"The soldiers called them Injuns, Pa. Why can't I?"

Rafe stood up. "People talk differently out here, Son. That doesn't mean we have to. We've covered a lot of ground today. Help your Ma get things cleaned up and I'll get your tent set up. We'll get an early start in the morning before it gets so hot."

"No need to set up my tent. I'll sleep with you under the wagon."

And sleep they did—so sound they didn't hear the stranger who walked into camp and added a few sticks to the fire to warm up the leftover coffee.

DORA WAS the first to awaken but she lay there for a moment listening to the muffled sound coming from outside the wagon. But then it stopped. From where she'd slept, she noted that the sky was showing the first signs of gray. It would be another thirty minutes until sunup so she may as well rest a while longer. As she lay there, she felt a light flutter in her lower abdomen, and she spread her hand tightly against it to see if it happened again. It didn't, but she'd noticed over the last few days that her waistline was thickening, and her dresses were a little tighter. She wanted to ask Rafe if he'd noticed but she didn't want to get his hopes up. It was a week past that critical period, but still too early to be optimistic, or was it?

She remembered the scripture in the 8th chapter of Matthew that Rafe often read. *And he saith unto them, Why are ye fearful, O ye of little faith? Then he arose and rebuked the winds and the sea; and there was a great calm.*

It was one of her husband's favorite verses to read when he was discouraged or worried about the crops. A feeling of joy coursed through her as she felt the flutter again. It was still too early to tell Rafe. He would try to make her take it easy, and there was too much work to do for that. She would keep this blessed secret tucked away in her heart.

She heard the sound again coming from outside. It was a familiar sound she remembered from childhood. Had Rafe taken up snoring? He'd teased her often enough for the whistling sound she made sometimes when sleeping on her back. She smiled. Now it was time to give him a little ribbing of his own. She sat up and gazed at her reflection in the small hand mirror she kept in her sewing basket. Her hairbrush was there too, and she pulled it through her hair as she did each morning upon rising, this time having to tug with a little more force than usual. Even though she'd washed it the evening before they left the fort, the dust and the dry, arid air had left it lackluster and frizzled. She put the brush and mirror back in the box. There was nothing to be done except tolerate it.

She sighed as she looked down at the ground from the back of the wagon. Tom had forgotten to put the stool there for her to step down. She lowered herself to a sitting position and was about to jump down when she saw a strange horse tied to a mesquite bush. She pulled her head and feet back in and grabbed Tom's rifle from the floor. She stuck her head out again, carefully this time. To the left of the campfire there was a strange man leaned against a saddle, sleeping. It was his snoring she'd heard. As soon as she'd eased down with the rifle in her hand, she nudged Rafe's foot with her own. It startled him and when he raised up, his head bumped underneath the wagon. The sound woke up the sleeping man and he raised his hands when he saw a Winchester boring down on him.

"Ma'am, don't shoot that thing. I don't mean no harm. I figured I'd be up and gone before you stirred around this mornin' but I guess I was more done-in than I thought. All I wanted was a cup of coffee and a place to rest my head. Your camp looked safe enough."

She lowered the rifle. "Well, I reckon if you'd meant to harm us, you could've done it easy enough in the night. No use to get all worked up about it now."

Rafe and Tom were now on their feet. The stranger did the same, but Dora noticed that he did it with a lot more difficulty. He's no spring chicken, she thought.

Rafe shook the dust off his clothes and reached down to pull on his boots.

"I'd check them boots for critters before I'd put 'em on," the old man said casually as he watched. "You're in desert country now, and many a man's been stung by a scorpion while slippin' a boot on in a hurry."

Rafe and Tom both checked their boots and then slipped them on their feet. "You musta' been done-in too, letting me slip up on you like that. You better watch your back—not everybody out here is as agreeable as me."

It irritated Rafe some that the old man had called him out, but he knew he was right. They had left civilization behind when they left the fort and from now on, he'd need to be more careful.

"I see what you mean," he said. "I'm Rafe McCade and this here is my boy, Tom." He pointed to Dora and grinned. "And I see you've already met my wife, Dora."

"Yep," he said, dusting his hat off and putting it on his head. "At the end of a gun barrel. It appears I'm the one needing to be more careful." He nodded his head at Dora. "Howdy, ma'am. I'm Billy Reed. You can just call me Billy—everybody else does."

"Billy, I'm pleased to meet you. We're heading out early this morning, but you can share our breakfast if you'll build up the fire."

Billy looked over at Rafe and grinned. "Ain't that just like a woman," he said, "always telling a man what to do."

"And you'd better hop to it," Rafe said, grinning back. "She's used to getting her way."

"Nothing wrong with giving a woman her way," he said. "She's gonna take it anyway and you may as well let her think it's your idea." He paused. When he spoke again, the light in his eyes had dimmed. "Had me a good woman once."

Dora sensed his sadness. "What happened, Billy?" she asked softly.

He hesitated so long, Dora wished she hadn't asked, but he finally spoke. "I didn't marry until I was fifty. She was a widow woman—lost her sorry, no account man in a gunfight. She was young, not quite thirty-five, but she took a liking to me. Said it was because I was kind. I'd been a rough and tumble man—never considered myself kind, but I wasn't mean like the man she'd had. We built up a nice little spread south of here and I'd rode down to the wash behind our place one morning to round up some strays. A new calf was stuck in some brush and it took me a while to free her. I was heading back home when I smelled smoke. Then I saw it and I knew where it was coming from. I lit out as fast as my old horse would carry me." He closed his eyes as if the memory was painful. "But I was too late. My Rebecca lay dead next to the corral with an arrow in her neck. They killed my woman and my baby that was inside her and then they burned my house."

Dora turned white. She thought of her own baby and how frightened his wife must have been for her own sake and for the sake of their baby. "Oh, I'm sorry," she said. "I shouldn't have asked."

"No ma'am. I led up to it." He saw how white Dora had turned. "I hope I didn't upset you too much by telling the story like that. It's been a long time—nigh on eight years—it don't hurt nearly as much as it used to." He smiled sadly. "But enough talking. If I don't get that fire laid out, we ain't never gonna eat breakfast and I'm hungrier than a jack-belly rabbit."

. . .

THE MAN NAMED Billy rode with them for three days and regaled them with tales of life on the Western frontier. Rafe thought his stories were somewhat embellished with each telling, but Tom was fascinated, and it relieved his boredom. Each morning Tom asked if he could ride the horse alongside Billy and Rafe let him. He gave all of them useful information they would need to know if they were to call this wild, uninhibited country home.

It wasn't till the second day that Billy recounted that he'd gone after the Indians who had killed his wife. "After I buried my wife, I took after 'em but they got wind of me somehow and there was a time or two that I was the one being hunted. When you're trying to evade an Indian, boy—now listen up because there might come a time when these words will come in handy—you got to think like an Indian. You'll need to brush out your back trail and you can't build no fire. They can smell the tiniest whiff of smoke a mile away."

"Did you ever catch up to them?" Tom asked, his eyes wide.

"I did. They were leading my two best horses. I'd know the tracks of that zebra dun anywhere. She'd lost half her shoe and I'd not had time to put on another one. The Injuns had lost me, so they just naturally thought I'd hightailed it out of there."

"What did you do when you found them?" Tom asked.

"Let's just say I got my horses back and their horses too. I'll leave it at that and spare you the details." Tom mulled it over in his mind. He knew what happened to those Indians—he wondered if Pa would have done the same if they'd killed Ma. It gave him chills to think on it—he found himself wishing they were already tucked away safely on Uncle Colin's ranch.

They rode ahead of the wagon and twice Billy stopped to let the wagon catch up. The thicket of blackjack oak was left behind. The first time they stopped, Billy pointed out how the vegetation had changed. The desert grasslands were before them with small stands of trees.

"If you'll pay attention to the plants, you can spare yourself some trouble. These mesquite trees here are close to thirty feet tall. As you go farther out in the desert where it rains less, they don't grow as tall. The grasses change too. It'll thin out, and before you know it, there won't be nothin' left but a few brown clumps here and there. By that time, you need to be hunting water if you plan to keep going."

"Where do you find water in the desert?" Tom asked.

"If you see willow trees, you'll know you're near a watering hole. Or sometimes you'll see a patch of barley growing. Pay attention to animal tracks and insects, especially bees. They'll take you straight to water. Some of the desert plants have water, like the prickly pear and the barrel cactus, but some of the others are poisonous so you've got to know your plants. We'll be on the watch and I'll point 'em out. There's a stretch of giant saguaros up ahead."

"What's a saguaro?"

"It's a cactus with arms reaching for the sky. They absorb water during the rainy season and one arm can weigh up to 500 pounds."

Tom looked at him skeptically.

"It's true, boy. They're filled with water. If you're in a bind you can take a sip, but it'll make you sick if you drink more than a sip or two. You can eat the fruit and it's right tasty, but it's hard to get at since it grows at the very top of the arms."

"But the best way to find water is to listen to people talk. Injuns know where the water is if they're a mind to tell you. There are a few old-timers around—desert rats I call 'em—and they'll tell a man where to find water. And I've known an outlaw or two who knows the desert well, but nobody knows it better than an Indian, and you can bet your last dollar that he'll be at the waterin' hole before you get there." He picked up some sand and let it run through his fingers. "The desert's a raw and wild place, boy. Best thing to do is avoid it if you can."

The next time he stopped, he pointed to some animal prints cutting straight across the trail. "Do you see these tracks?"

Tom got down from the horse and studied the tracks. "Looks like a dog's tracks," he said.

Billy got down too. "They're coyote tracks. A dog's got wider feet. A coyote track is long and narrow. This one was chasing something."

"What do they eat?" Tom asked, examining the print.

"Lizards, rabbits, insects; they'll even eat cactus fruit and the bean pods from the mesquite if they can't find meat."

"What I want to see is a herd of buffalo."

"You won't have to wait long. Dry season is coming, and they'll be heading north. Maybe tomorrow or the next day."

"Will you be riding with us all the way to Willow Bar, Billy?"

"I'll ride one more day with you, but late tomorrow I'll be taking the southeast fork and head home." He looked in the direction of the wagon. "Your ma and pa are about to catch up. I'm hoping she's got some of those biscuits left from breakfast. Riding makes a man hungry."

"Yes Sir," Tom said, sitting up in the saddle a little higher. "Riding does make a man hungry."

Billy noticed the subtle difference in the boy's manner and nodded. "A boy becomes a man in a hurry out here, son. You're asking good questions and listening. Don't ever think you know more than a man who's been long in the saddle. The way to manhood is to always be learning something new and doing what's got to be done."

"Like you done to those Indians?"

"I never held much to killing anything I don't plan to eat. Never shot a bird unless I was going to make a meal out of it. But what those Injuns done to my wife, they deserved what they got. There's not much in the way of law out here yet, son, and until there is, we got to take the law into our own hands. Those were renegades, broke off from their tribe, and they're the worst lot. Not all Injuns are bad. They just don't have white man's ways and they don't think like us. A lot of men are going to get killed trying to make peace with the Indian because they don't understand 'em. But it ain't just the Injuns you got to be worried about. There's evil lurking in the hearts of white men too."

Tom thought about telling Billy about his pa having to kill the river pirate to protect Clay, but ma had said be careful who you tell things to. He didn't feel much like tellin' it anyway. He still had nightmares about it. He had been wondering exactly what it meant to be evil though. Maybe Billy would know.

"How do you tell who's evil?" he asked. "My Uncle Aiden is a mean-spirited man. Does that make him evil?

"No, there's a difference. My own pa was mean-spirited but he wadn't evil. You'll know evil when you come upon it. Just use the good sense God gave you. If you've got a funny feeling about somebody, make a wide circle around 'em."

The wagon had caught up. "Whoa up," Rafe said to the horses. He jumped to the ground and then helped Dora down.

"I'll fix us a bite to eat," she said. "I figured you stopped because you're hungry."

Billy rubbed his stomach and looked at Tom. "That's downright uncanny, boy. That Ma of yours can read a man's mind."

After the meal, Rafe rode ahead with Billy while Tom and Dora followed behind them in the wagon. By mid-afternoon, it was so hot, they decided to stop for the day while they still had shade from the mesquite trees. They would bed early and start at 3 am the next morning.

The dried beans Dora had been soaking in a crock in the back of the wagon all day were now simmering in a kettle over the campfire. "I wish we had some fresh meat to go with these beans," she said to Rafe when he finished bringing in more fuel for the fire.

"I thought the same, but Billy said it would be best not to fire a gun. He said we might get some unwanted attention. I guess he was talking about Indians."

"Why don't you cut a few slices off the bacon then. Beans don't seem like much of a meal."

"No need to do that," Billy said, walking up to the camp holding two large quail. "I'll dress these, and we can put 'em on a spit."

"Where did those come from?" Rafe asked. "I didn't hear you shoot."

"I shot alright," Billy said with a big grin on his face. "Just not with a gun." He pulled a slingshot from the back of his pocket. "A quail is a lazy bird. I snuck up on 'em Injun style and they didn't know what hit 'em."

. . .

"FOR IT TO HAVE BEEN SO HOT during the day, it sure is cool out here tonight," Dora said as they all settled around the fire after they'd eaten.

"That's the way of the desert, ma'am," Billy said. "It's got lots of strange ways and a man has got to learn to adapt to 'em or he won't live long." He pulled a splinter off the nearest piece of firewood and began to pick his teeth. A long-forgotten memory came to the surface of Dora's mind. The hastily made toothpick was something her father would do in their cabin back in the hills of Tennessee. She smiled at the thought and listened as the weather-worn man in front of her told his tales.

"There's people who've been found dead in the desert less than two hundred yards from water and them not knowin' it. Course we're not in the desert proper yet, just on the edge of it. Before this trail was mapped out, lots of folks took a wrong turn. Some survived to tell about it; some didn't." By this time Billy had rolled up a smoke. He took the splinter he'd used for a toothpick, held it briefly to the fire and lit the cigarette, then threw the flaming tinder back into the fire.

"Knew a young fellow once; Corbin was his name, although he couldn't ever remember if it was his first name or his last name. Prob'ly from the shock of all the things that happened to 'im. Anyways his family's wagon trailed way out in the desert and Indians attacked 'em. They killed all but young Corbin. Indians will do that sometimes if they sense that a boy has spunk in 'im. They raised him like their own, but he never got over the death of his family and he lit out on his own when he wasn't but a couple years older than Tom here."

Billy drew on his smoke and let his breath out while the others waited for his story to continue. "That Corbin knew the ways of the desert like no other. Knew where every waterin' hole was and knew how to bring one back to life if it wadn't there when he got to it."

"How do you do that?" Tom asked.

"In a dry year, the water can seem to be all dried up, but if you dig deep enough, you can get enough of a trickle to water your horse and fill your canteen."

"Where's this Corbin now?" Dora asked.

"I've not heard from him in quite a while now. Some say he has a mining claim up in the hills somewhere and shows up every now and then down in Placerville to cash in his gold. Wherever it is, there must be a good bit of it. Folks have tried following him, but the tracks run out after a while. It's like he disappears into thin air, some say."

"Speaking of folks," he said, "you'll find all kinds of men out here; some of the best and some of the worst. You might find an educated man from the east driving cattle to settle on a ranch in New Mexico. A man who can read and write can study up on a few law books and become a lawyer. An animal doctor back east might become a good old sawbones doctor in a Western town. I once heard of a blacksmith from Missouri stopping his wagon and building up an entire town by setting up shop, then helping others that came with him do the same. A man comes into his own when he gets out here. He develops skills he never knew he had because he never needed 'em before. You'll find good men and bad men—some of both hiding behind a badge. Some become lawmen because it's the honorable thing to do, and some do it for the benefits that being above the law can bring. You'll find men that will do everything they can to help you along, and you'll find 'em that will take everything you've got—even your life if they've half a mind to. And sometimes it's hard to tell the difference. An evil heart is easy to hide with a handshake and a smile, so my advice is not to trust anybody until you know what's on their mind."

"But we trusted you," Tom said.

"I'd already showed that it wasn't my intention to harm you. It's a good thing it was me who come along 'cause you were an easy target setting up camp without a guard watching. You've been able to get away with that until now, but from here on out, you'll need to keep a careful eye out on things. Don't let your guard down."

It had been a pleasant way to pass the evening and Rafe was grateful to have Billy keep watch for part of the night. They made coffee and ate venison jerky for breakfast the next morning. The sun was still three hours from rising when they broke camp and started on their way.

It was nearly noon when they heard what they'd all been waiting for. It was just like Billy had told them. They heard the ground rumbling long before they saw the sea of buffalo appear on the horizon.

"Hurry," Billy said. "We need to drop back amongst those rocks we just passed. They're heading this way and there'll be some Indians alongside them."

They did as he suggested and watched in awe as the massive beasts thundered by not more than three hundred yards away from their position. The whoops and yells from the Indians were drowned out by the deafening sound of the hoofbeats. Dust from the upended sand was flying everywhere and they covered their mouths and noses to keep from breathing it in.

Dora's heart was pounding as hard as the hoofbeats when they finally passed. "That was something to behold," she said as the last of the beasts went out of sight. "I never heard such a whoopin' and a hollerin'. How many buffalo do you think there were, Billy?"

"I don't rightly know," he said. "At least a thousand if I had to guess. I've seen bigger herds, but this is the most I've seen this late in the season."

"Did the Indians see us?" Tom asked, barely able to contain his excitement.

"I doubt it; they were too intent on the herd. But it wouldn't have mattered if they did. Those were Jicarilla Apache, a peaceful tribe. They leave us alone as long as we leave them alone."

"I'm glad we got to see 'em; the buffalo, I mean. They came so close. What if we'd been out there in the middle of 'em?"

"Wouldn't have been much left to identify," Billy said with a grin, "just some buttons off our shirts and maybe a belt buckle or two. They would have tried to avoid the wagon, but with so many of them bunched together like that, there's not much they can do to stop. When they're running, they have the herd mentality. Where one goes, the rest follow."

They hated to have Billy leave them when they stopped for camp later in the afternoon. They had made camp and were drinking coffee.

"I wish you'd stay for supper," Dora said as she refilled their cups.

"There ain't nothing that I'd rather do than have another fine meal prepared by your hands, ma'am. You're a good cook and I'd be trying to steal you away from Rafe here if he wasn't such a decent sort of fellow." When he grinned, the lines along his wrinkled cheeks grinned with him.

Dora blushed. "Well, you'll need something to eat to take with you," she said as she busied herself near the fire.

"I'll be home before dark, but if you've got a cold biscuit to spare, I'll take it along to eat with the jerky."

"They're yesterday's biscuits," she said. "You might have to break one on a rock before you can eat it." She went to the back of the wagon and came back with three biscuits wrapped in a piece of the brown paper the clerk from the army base had used to pack their bacon in.

"I appreciate it, ma'am," he said, tipping his hat to her.

"If you're ever near Big Sandy, stop in to see us," Rafe said as Billy tightened the cinch on his saddled horse."

"I might just do that," he said. He turned to Tom. "I'd like to see what kind of man this one grows up to be. He's got fine makings for turning into a good one." He reached inside the pocket of his vest and pulled out something wrapped in velvety cloth. "I've got a present for you, boy. It was something I planned to give my own son one day, but it must'a not been in the Lord's plan for me to have a boy of my own." He unwrapped the cloth and pulled out a shiny object dangling from a chain.

"It was my uncle's watch." He held it up so that the sun filtering through the mesquite shone upon it. "When my ma and pa died, me and my sister went to live with my uncle. He didn't have children of his own, so he was glad to take us in." He looked at Rafe. "You may have heard of him," he said with another infectious smile. "Samuel Huntington. He was once the governor of Connecticut."

Rafe's eyes grew wide. "And a signer of the Constitution," he said, nodding his head. "What made you come out west when you could have lived in luxury back east. Didn't you inherit his estate?"

"We did, but it was contested by some others in the family. He had another brother and some nephews. When Uncle Sam died, I didn't want to be part of the bickering, so I came out here to start a new life. He gave us an education and a good upbringing. I didn't need much else. Sam was a good man and he would want his watch to go to a good man in the making. Besides, if I keep it, it's liable to end up alongside my scalp on the loop of some Indian's war stick. I'd rather you have it," he said, folding the cloth and handing it to Tom.

Tom took it out and examined the watch's fine craftsmanship. He had never seen anything so fancy. He looked at his pa waiting to see if he would let him keep it.

"I don't know what to say, Billy," Rafe said. "You could sell this watch and get a good bit of money for it."

"What's money when you've got no one to share it with," he said. And with that, he lifted his foot into the stirrup and mounted his horse. "Make your pa proud, son," he said, and with those words he was gone.

The next day they would be in Willow Bar, pick up a few supplies and then be looking on the long end of trouble.

CHAPTER TWELVE
TRAIL TO NOWHERE

The desert sky had not quite lost its rosy glow when Rafe poured the last bit of kerosene into the lantern. He knew this same sky that had been so bright during the heat of the day would turn pitch black just minutes after sunset, and the never-ending sea of sand offered little fuel for a campfire. They'd stepped into it, alright. Trouble with a capital T.

Dora came from the back of the wagon. "You better light out, Rafe. Me and Tom will be fine." She handed him a buckskin bag and a canteen. "I've packed you some biscuits and jerky. It'll keep you from being hungry."

Rafe set the lantern down on the sand. He slung the bag and canteen over his left shoulder and pulled Dora into a tender hug. "I don't want to leave you and the boy here by yourselves. I'm sorry I got us in this mess."

She reached up and brushed the hair out of his eyes. "Aw, hush now—we'll be alright." She hoped she sounded convincing enough. Truth be told, she was scared.

Rafe caressed her soft, smooth face with his rough, calloused hand and then turned away quickly before he changed his mind. The sun was just setting so he pointed himself in that direction and started walking. Canyon Springs was at least fourteen miles to the northwest. With an even terrain, he could be there in five or six hours, but the sand was anything but even. On foot, he would be lucky to be there before dawn.

Now and again he studied the sky. It wouldn't do for him to get turned around out here with no landmarks to go by. He knew Canyon Springs lay somewhere between the star to the North and the two bright stars to the West. He figured he had gone about two miles by now, but it was hard to judge—it was slower going than he'd figured on. The afternoon's mishap had taken a toll on his boots and he had to stop often to shake the sand out from the flaps.

He thought about Dora and Tom and wondered if they were scared. He could have kicked himself for listening to those two drifters they had met when they stopped in Willow Bar for supplies. And he'd done it even though Billy had warned him about trusting people. Dora didn't like the looks of 'em—said they were starin' at her like she was a saloon girl. Even in her long skirts, Dora had always turned heads. Rafe still thought she was the prettiest woman he'd ever seen, and he wondered again how she had been attracted to him in the first place.

The drifters had told him of a shortcut. "You'll skirt the desert, but there's plenty of water," the one called Mort said. "It'll save you two days ride." It was the thought of saving two days' ride that appealed to Rafe. He wondered why Colin hadn't mentioned the shortcut, but maybe it was something new. The men seemed to know what they were talking about, so after Rafe got what they needed in town, they made camp on the bank of a creek a few miles out of town and the next morning he took off in the direction the men had pointed out.

It was an old trail and looked good enough to begin with but after a few hours it fizzled out and there was nothing left but ruts left by wagon wheels of long ago. Rafe started to turn back but kept going in hopes of picking up the trail to the north that the men had mentioned. Maybe he'd missed it. They hadn't met a soul coming or going so there was no one to ask. He'd looked back once and thought he saw dust from other horses, but nothing ever came of it. Whoever it was didn't want to be seen, whether Indian or white. And that's what concerned Rafe. It meant they were up to no good. Billy had warned him, and he'd been a fool not to take heed.

The trouble had started later in the afternoon. Sand drifts had covered a patch of black lava—sharp as glass it was—and the horses were on it before Rafe realized the lava was there. The rock was sharp and jagged, and he could tell by the gait of the horses that they were suffering. A quick inspection of their feet told him all he needed to know. They were cut up pretty bad. Rafe's tattered boots hadn't fared so well either.

When he finally got the horses on soft sand, he saw that their feet were going to need some patching up before they could continue to pull the wagon. It worried him that they might be ruined for good. It'd be a shame. He'd raised those horses from birth, and they were of fine stock. He'd considered riding the mare to Canyon Springs, but she was in bad shape too and he didn't want to risk her going lame. Some men wouldn't worry so much over a horse, but it wasn't in Rafe's nature to abuse one.

Walking had given him time to think on it and now he was mad. "Those boys sent me on a trail to nowhere," he said aloud. The sound of his own voice startled him; it was different out in the middle of a barren desert with nothing for it to bounce off of.

He plodded on and said a small prayer that there would be horses available in Canyon Springs and that he would have enough money to pay for them. He should be there before dawn if he kept up his pace. He'd have to keep a watchful eye on the stars. Billy had told him about the bones of men lost in the desert being found years later, any identification having been blown away by the wind. That's not how he wanted to end up. He had Dora and Tom to think about.

The more Rafe thought about the men back in Willow Bar, the more uneasy he became. If they knew the country like they said, why hadn't they warned him about the lava? He stopped abruptly. Unless they knew the horses would get in trouble! They would also know it would be Rafe that would have to leave and find help. Why, those sorry no accounts had probably planned it all out! Dora and Tom would be nearly defenseless all alone out there in the desert with no place to hide. Except for the small outcropping of rocks near the wagon, there was nothing but sand.

Dora would have built a fire by now with the buffalo chips she and Tom had picked up and stored under the wagon along the way. They would be sittin' ducks with that fire burning bright. Could be I'm wrong, he thought, but in his mind, he knew he wasn't. He was no tenderfoot, but any man can make mistakes and he knew now he'd figured those drifters wrong. The moon was just a smile in the sky, but between the light from it and the stars, he could see well enough without the lantern. He lowered the wick until the flame was out. Without giving it any more thought, he turned swiftly around and didn't waste any time following the tracks he'd just made.

DORA BUILT up a fire soon after Rafe left and the smell of coffee brewing in the pot was comforting. There was no need to fix supper with Rafe gone so she and Tom made do with leftover biscuits and a jar of honey.

If they just hadn't met those two scoundrels in Willow Bar, they wouldn't be in this mess. She hadn't trusted 'em one bit, but Rafe was so set on getting to Colin's place that he hadn't used sound judgment when sizing up their character. Morton and Hatch had been their names—shiftier fellers she'd never seen. If only Rafe had listened to her this time. He usually did. He'd even been warned by Billy about men with evil in their hearts.

It was different being out here without Rafe—spooky even. Tom was good company, but even though he'd growed up a right smart along the way, he wasn't yet a man. After a while, she pulled her blanket a little closer and leaned back against the wheel, close enough to the fire to stay warm but not so close as to be seen right away should someone come up without warning. But why would she think that? They had seen no one on the trail all day. She shrugged, trying to shake off the uneasiness she felt.

Tom scooted over beside her and she put her arm around him.

"It sure gets cold in a hurry when the sun goes down," he said. "I don't like it out here, Ma. It's spooky."

She laughed. "That's just what I was thinkin'. We're used to making camp in the shelter of trees instead of wide-open spaces," she said. "But you know what? There's no use dwellin' on what we can't change." She pointed to a star in the sky. "The stars are bright tonight. See that big one over yonder? It's watchin' over us and yer Pa at the same time. Kinda like the good Lord watches over all of us."

"Is that the direction Pa's going?"

"No, that's the North Star. He's going a little further to the west; thataway," she said, pointing her hand. "See those two stars right together? That's where he's headin'—Canyon Springs, it's called. We saw a sign a while back. He'll find horses there."

"What will we do with our horses?"

"We'll take 'em with us. They'll be able to walk some if they don't have a load to haul. The salve I rubbed on their feet will help but it'll take a few days to heal."

"I'd sure hate to lose 'em," Tom said. "We've been down some rough roads together."

She nodded. "That we have, son. Don't worry, they'll pull through. After they heal, we can sell the horses your pa buys." Tom relaxed and rested his head on her shoulder and she smiled. He was still her little boy, but he would soon be as tall as Rafe.

"Are you getting sleepy, son?"

"Yes, ma'am. I am."

"We'll go to bed when the fire dies down. Just rest easy."

She dozed off but sat up with a start when she heard a faint click of hooves as they briefly touched the lava. She listened closely. All was quiet, but the horses were uneasy and so was she. She'd learned to trust the instincts of their horses along the trail. The fire had died down some and they sat in the shadow of the water barrel mounted on the wagon. As if also sensing something was wrong, she felt a distinctive kick in her belly. Their baby had moved! Her maternal instinct took over and she felt a fierceness akin to a mother bear.

"Tom," she whispered, "get the Winchester out of the wagon and slip back behind those rocks away from the fire." Tom rose quietly from the sand. He did as he was told and no sooner had he got out of sight, two horses with riders rode in.

"Well now, little lady" said the man called Morton as he looked around the camp. "Looks like some fix you and your man got yourself into." Dora felt a chill that had nothing to do with the night air. She wrapped the blanket tighter around her.

"Fix?" she asked. "We ain't in no fix. We just stopped to make camp." She said it with more boldness than she felt.

She was hoping they'd keep riding. She groaned inwardly when they dismounted. Morton walked over to the horses and examined their hooves. "Looks like their horses are in trouble, don't it Hatch?"

Dora looked around at the smaller man, Hatch. He was leering at her with a toothless grin. "Where's your man and boy?" Morton asked as he looked about.

"They turned in early. We're all about tuckered out. Help yourself to the rest of the coffee before you ride on. But you're not welcome at our camp. You gave us some bad directions." She held her head up and tried to remain steady, but inside she was all tied up in knots.

"Is that so?" said Morton. "I was planning on telling your man that somehow I got mixed up and told you the wrong way to go. I didn't mean to lead you astray." He rubbed his hands over the fire. "I'll just go to the back of the wagon and rouse him."

MEANWHILE RAFE WAS MAKING BETTER time walking back. He had cut some strips off the buckskin bag and repaired his boots the best he could. He couldn't help but wonder what was going on back at the wagon. If those men caught Dora unawares, she and the boy would be in trouble. He picked up his speed.

. . .

DORA STIRRED UP THE FIRE. "Why don't you have some coffee before you wake my man up," she said. "Rafe's going to be mad as a hornet gittin' woke up after no more'n an hour's sleep."

She was trying to delay what they were aiming to do to her. Tom was a good shot and would do everything he could to protect her. Somehow, some way, she was going to save this baby.

"Lord, I need a miracle," she said aloud.

"What's that you said?" Mort asked.

"Just somethin' I always say," she said. "I was asking the good Lord to watch over us on this fine and starry night."

"Hmph," Hatch said, and sneered.

She picked up the coffee pot. It was then she saw the fork that Tom had used to dip out his honey. That boy, she thought—using a fork when he should have been using a spoon—and would he never learn to put things away? She grabbed the fork up. This time she was glad he hadn't. It wasn't much but she slipped it into her lace-up shoe and said another prayer.

"Coffee?" she asked again.

Mort grinned. "Why not? We ain't in much of a hurry." He reached for the cup she was holding out.

TOM'S HANDS were steady as he got the bigger man in the sights of the Winchester. He had killed rabbits, squirrels and deer with it, but killing a man was different. He thought again how bothered Pa had been when he'd had to shoot the river pirate. He'd had a gun then too, but Ma and Pa had been there to back him up. There was nobody but him now. Pa was half-way to nowhere.

He was scared. As he leaned back against the rock, he could still feel the day's heat radiating from it. A small lizard scurried over the rock in front of him and dropped down into the sand. The diversion calmed him down some. I've got a man's job to do, he thought. I'm not going to let 'em hurt Ma. His jaw hardened as he looked down the barrel.

RAFE SAW the bright glow of the campfire from a distance away. Like the stars that had guided him out of camp, the small glow of the fire was guiding him in, but it worried him that it was still burning strong. Dora should have gone to bed by now. As he closed in, he made for the rock outcropping hoping to remain hidden until he could see what was happening. Just as he got to the rocks, he saw that his hunch was right. The two men were there alright, and the one called Hatch was looking in the back of the wagon. He heard him yell out, "Her man ain't in the wagon, Mort."

DORA TRIED to move away from the fire but not before Mort grabbed her by the arm. Where was Tom? Was he in the back of the wagon or had he slipped off in the rocks like she'd told him to? She hoped and prayed he was out of harm's way.

Mort laughed as he held Dora's arms behind her back. "So, they both went off and left you out here all by your lonesome, did they? Well, we'll keep you good company, won't we Hatch?" He started dragging her towards the wagon.

Dora tried to visual the contents of the wagon and what she might use as a weapon. She'd made her mind up that she wasn't going to let what happened to Billy's wife happen to her.

RAFE'S BLOOD WAS BOILING. Dora would be scared out of her mind, but he knew she would fight until he could get to her. Right now he needed to know where Tom was. He heard a faint shuffling from the rocks beside him.

"Pa, over here." It was Tom's voice and he was whispering.

"Glad you're ok, boy—I've got to go in and help your ma before they hurt her."

Tom sighed with relief that he wasn't alone. "I had my sights set on the big one, but then he grabbed her. I can't shoot now for fear of hitting Ma."

"You did good boy. I'll go around and come in from the other side of the wagon. You keep your gun on the short one and I'll take care of the one that's got your ma."

Hatch was sitting at the fire drinking his coffee when he heard Dora scream. He grinned and stoked the fire.

Rafe reached the wagon just as he heard his wife cry out. He pulled back the curtain and Mort turned around in surprise. He started to lunge for Rafe but stopped suddenly, let out a yelp and fell out of the wagon on his face with a fork plunged deep between his shoulder blades. Hatch heard the commotion from where he sat and ran for the back of the wagon. A shot rang out and Hatch stopped short, then fell over top of Mort.

RAFE TOOK his time hitching up the horses while Tom set about filling the water bucket from their barrel to give them one last drink before they set out again. The injured horses would follow behind the wagon while the other two, along with the horses that belonged to Mort and Hatch would be pulling the heavy load of the wagon.

Dora filled a canteen and set it between the two drifters sitting with their backs against the rocks. One was a mite pale and the other had a bandage where his ear had once been. "You'll work those ropes off in a day or two," she said. "Might even be before the buzzards find you or maybe it won't." She checked the ropes. "I wouldn't count on it, though. My Rafe now; he ties the meanest knots I've ever seen."

Mort looked up pleadingly at Dora. "We'll die out here, ma'am. I'm hurt bad. Just turn us loose. We won't be troublin' you again." She looked over at Hatch. He wasn't leering anymore.

"Don't be ma'aming me. Last night you were aimin' to kill me, so I don't have any sympathy for you at all."

"At least take this fork out of my back," Mort said. "It'll get infection in it if you don't."

"And you might bleed to death if I do," she said. "It's staying right where it is. The only reason I bandaged that one's ear is I figured the buzzards would peck his brains out if I didn't."

They both looked horrified at the thought. Rafe was still hoppin' mad over what they may have done to Dora if he hadn't got back in time. He realized now that sometimes killing a man is justified if you fear for the lives of those you love. These men were unarmed and no longer posing a danger, but it wouldn't hurt for him to scare them a little.

He pulled out his pistol. "I've a mind to shoot you anyway for what you put my woman through last night."

A new fear came over their faces. "Ma'am, I beg you. You can't just let him shoot us while we're tied up like this."

"You should'a thought better of it back in Willow Bar when you gave us the wrong directions." She shook the last bits of sand from the blankets and put them in the back of the wagon. "Put your gun up, Rafe. They ain't worth the bullets you'd be wastin'. They'll have plenty of time to ponder upon their sinful ways with the sun bearing down on them about midday."

Rafe grinned as he tightened the last strap. Dora was going to make those boys wish they were dead. "Up you go," he said as he lifted her into the seat of the wagon and took up the reins. "Ma'am," he said, with a smile of mischief, "I'll do whatever you say. Just don't ask me to walk across that desert again until I get me a new pair of boots."

She looked down at his boots that were held together by nothing but leather strips and laughed. She brushed her lips against his weathered cheek. "You can ma'am me all you want, Rafe McCade," she said. "I think I'll keep you around." Tom climbed into the back and pulled the rawhide curtain to keep the sand out.

Dora called out to the two men. "You don't deserve it, but we'll send the sheriff from the next town out here to see how you're holdin' up," she said.

"Or maybe we won't," Tom called out between the curtains. Rafe chuckled at the expressions on the faces of Morton and Hatch. He would make sure someone came out to get them by tomorrow. No matter how no-account they were, he was a better man than to let them die of thirst in the desert.

He lifted the reins urging the horses to go forward. It was time to head back and pick up the trail. They wouldn't have to go all the way back to Willow Bar but would pick up the trail to Raton's Pass as they should have done the first time around.

CHAPTER THIRTEEN
RATON'S PASS

With each plod of the horse's hooves, they left the desert behind them and by late afternoon they were coming up on Raton's Pass. It wasn't a town at all, just a lonely trading post and a relay station. Rafe was glad to see a blacksmith had set up shop in a lean-to off the side of the relay station and he stopped the wagon there.

Tom was looking at the trading post with interest. "Can we go inside, Pa?"

"Help me unhitch the horses and you and your ma can go in. I'll feed and water them and then talk to the smithy."

The corral where the relay horses were kept had two watering troughs, so he led all the horses over to it. There was a bundle of hay nearby and the horses took a particular interest in it.

"Who do I pay for the hay?" Rafe hollered out to the blacksmith.

"It's my hay. Just feed 'em and you can pay me later," he shouted back.

"I'll need your services too," he said. "I've got some problems here."

"I'll be right there."

"We ran into a mite of trouble on the trail," Rafe said as the blacksmith examined the horses he was leading. "These two were on the front and they're worse off than the others."

"Looks like you ran into some lava rock by the way they're cut up," he said, looking up at Rafe.

"I'm afraid so."

His expression was thoughtful as he looked into Rafe's eyes. "Let me guess. Someone told you of a shortcut?"

Rafe showed his surprise. "How did you know?"

"It's happened before. You're just lucky you lived to tell about. Some haven't."

"But for the grace of God, my wife wouldn't have," Rafe said. I started off on foot after some new horses, but something told me to turn around and go back."

"There's a US marshal inside the relay station right now. He's been looking for those fellows for months now, but they always slip away. No tracks, no nothing."

"They won't be slipping away no more," Rafe said. "They're tied up right where we left 'em back on the lava rocks this morning. They'll be sunbaked and thirsty right about now. One's missing his left ear where my boy shot it off with his rifle and the other has a good-sized fork stuck in his back where my wife stabbed him. I tied 'em up pretty tight. I don't think there's any chance they'll be getting loose anytime soon."

"Lord 'a mercy, man. I wouldn't want to tangle with you folks."

"Like I said, it was my wife and boy that really did 'em in. You sure don't want to tangle with my woman," he said with a big grin on his face. "She's a good one to ride the trail with."

"That little bitty thing that walked in the store?"

"She might be little, but she's tough when the need arises."

"There's a bounty on those boys' heads. You might wanna talk to the marshal about it."

"That's good to know. If my horses are ruined, I'll need to buy some new ones. The two paints over there belong to those no-good scoundrels that tricked us."

The blacksmith wiped his hands on his apron. "If they're ruined, I'd say you'd be justified in trading horses with 'em." He held his right hand out to Rafe. "I'm Frank Polk. I'm sure I can get 'em fixed up for you."

"I hope you can, Frank. They've been with us all the way. They come from good stock."

"I can see they do." He examined the cuts again. "At least their hooves ain't cracked. That's a good sign. And I don't see any sign of infection. They're not as bad as most horses I've tended to for what they've been through." He sniffed as he held the horse's leg. "What's that smell?"

"My wife's good at doctorin'. It's a salve she made up this morning before we headed out."

"Looks like it's working. Do you know what's in it?"

Rafe glanced up to see Dora and Tom walk out of the store with a package. "There she is now." She was walking toward the wagon. "Dora," he called out. She turned her head. "Come over here, will you?"

She nodded and handed the package to Tom. "Put this in the wagon, son."

She walked over to Rafe's side. "What is it? Are the horses alright?"

"They will be," he said. "Frank here wants to know what kind of concoction you made up to put on their feet."

"I mixed up some liquorice, mint and yarrow with lanolin," she said, looking up at Rafe.

"That's a right curious combination," the smithy said, "but they're healing so good I might give it a try. The trading post has liquorice and lanolin, but I'll have to send off for mint. I've never heard of this yarrow."

"I don't know if it grows out here," she said. "Indians use it back home—it's good medicine for wounds. I've got a little I can spare. I just throw things together based on the little bit I know—sometimes they work, sometimes they don't."

"I appreciate it," he said. "It'll take me an hour or two to get the horses shod. You want me to do all four? They need it."

"Yes, please, and the mare too. None of them have been shod since we left the fort."

"I'll take care of 'em. You can go into the relay station. He's got an Indian woman that cooks for 'im. This is the time of day she starts rustling up some grub. That's what the marshal is hanging around for."

"I'm all for it," Dora said. "I'm tired of eating my own cooking."

Rafe looked down at his feet. "But first I need to go into the trading post before I walk right out of these boots."

THE MARSHAL WAS sure enough interested in the boys they'd left behind on the lava rock. "Mort and Hatch, that's them alright," he said when Rafe told him what had happened. "Charlie Morton and Cliff Hatchell—outlaws in the worst kind of way. They're wanted for horse thievin' and robbing an army payroll. The big one named Morton is wanted for having his way with a woman which is a hanging offense out here for certain. He almost killed the woman, so you're lucky, ma'am," he said to Dora.

"The Lord had his hand in it," she said. "And Rafe came back just in the nick of time."

Just thinking about how close Dora had come to being hurt got Rafe worked up all over again. "If he'd done any harm to Dora, he'd be a dead man now," he told the marshal. "He might be anyway with that fork still stuck in his back."

The marshal laughed. "I guess I best be riding out that way after I finish supper. Coyotes might take a shine to 'em and there won't be enough left to identify 'em for the reward money. Will you be heading out tonight?" he asked.

"We'll spend the night here and head on out in the morning."

"How can I get you the reward money?"

"I'll be at my brother's place on Big Sandy Creek north of here. His name is Colin McCade."

"McCade's your brother?" he asked in astonishment.

"Yes, do you know him?"

"I'll say I do! I've been trying to make a lawman out of him, but he won't have nothing to do with it. Folks respect him out here and are hoping he'll go into politics when we get the territories settled."

"Colin? In politics? I can't believe that," he said with a lopsided grin.

"Well, believe it, 'cause it'll happen sooner or later."

The station master and the Indian girl he had hired on as a cook came out with heaping plates of food. "A home-cooked meal and I didn't have to cook it," Dora said. She took the first bite and the rest followed suit.

"By the way," Rafe asked as he shoveled a spoonful of food in his mouth. "How much is the bounty on those two?"

"It's not chicken feed," the marshal said. He gestured to the station master. "Harvey, do you still have those wanted posters?"

"I've got them right here," he said, snatching two papers off the wall near the door. He laid them on the table in front of Rafe. Rafe coughed, he sputtered, and Dora had to hit him on the back to keep him from choking on his food.

"That's $600 total," he said a few minutes later when he had composed himself.

"Well, they are serious offenses," the marshal said. "Hanging offenses. But you understand that I have to know they're still there before I can give you the money?"

"I understand. Someone could have come by and turned 'em loose."

"I doubt it. Not too many people wander out that way unless they've been misled like you were. I'll take 'em back to Santa

Fe. That's where I have to pick up the money anyway. Could be a couple of weeks, but I'll get it to you."

"Their horses are outside," Rafe said. "If those boys manage to get untied, they won't make it far on foot."

After they finished eating, the marshal headed out. Rafe got up to pay for their food.

"It's on me," Harvey said. "I'd pay money to hear a story like that and I'll be passing it on for a long time comin'." He walked to the table to pick up the plates and spoke to Dora. "You've got gumption, ma'am. I'll give you that."

Rafe left two dollars on the counter anyway. "Don't be tellin' her that," he said with a grin. "It'll go to her head."

"Our boy's the one with gumption," she said. "I'm right proud of him."

Tom puffed up a little bit, enjoying the attention. "I just did what I had to do," he said.

Dora smiled. He was getting more like his daddy every day.

"Well I'm proud you stopped in here. We need people with grit and gumption to settle out here." He picked up their plates. "Listen, I've got three bunks in the back room if you folks want to use 'em for tonight. Won't be another stage until tomorrow and I ain't expecting no guests." He carried the plates to the kitchen. "No charge. Clean sheets and everything. Take it or leave it," he said.

"We'll take it." Dora said. "Our mattress is full of sand. I hope to heaven I never see another desert."

Tom had gone right to sleep but the excitement of nearing the end of their journey kept Rafe and Dora awake for a while.

"We're so close," Dora said. "What do you think the ranch will be like? Is it a big place?"

"The way Colin described it, I don't think we'll have any close neighbors if that's what you mean."

"At least Tom will have their boy to play with," she said. "He's used to having his cousins back home."

"Tom will be good to the boy; I'm sure of that. You saw how he was with Clay's boy, Jimmy, and with Edward's boys. But I think he's gettin' a little old for kid's games. He'll be helpin' me quite a bit, anyway. He won't have much time for play."

"Yes, he's gettin' big, Rafe. He ain't the same little boy who left Kentucky."

"We've all grown from it, Dora—you more than any of us. I was worried about you starting on this trip. You were so frail for so long after we lost baby Alice. Does it hurt for me to bring her name up like that?"

"Not anymore. When I paid her grave a visit before we left, I had me a good talk with God and he gave me some peace about it. And I told your Ma to look after our girl in heaven and she whispered that she would."

"I don't doubt you heard her voice. You and Ma were always close like she was your own ma."

"I think the hardships we've been through have made me stronger. Who'da thought that little gal you brought home from the Tennessee hills would stand up to the likes of those river rats. We sure enough met up with some hard cases, didn't we?"

"We sure did. And who would have thought that little gal from Tennessee would earn enough in reward money to stake us a couple hundred head of cattle."

"It wadn't just me, Rafe. You've been sayin' it, but it ain't so. It was all of us workin' together."

"You could have fooled me," he said. "Anyway, you got more grit than any woman out here."

She yawned. "Turn down the lamp, Rafe. I'm gettin' sleepy."

He did and they were both asleep before you could count to twenty.

CHAPTER FOURTEEN
THE LAST CAMP

The next morning after breakfast at the relay station, the McCades left Raton's Pass behind. The horses were newly shod and raring to go. It had been a pleasant stop and with the anticipation of only a day's journey ahead and the prospect of the reward money coming, they started off with renewed energy and smiles on their faces.

The landscape changed almost as drastically as the temperature when they headed into a small mountain range a few miles north. They left the mesquite and sandhills behind as they climbed steadily into a higher elevation and a greener world. By the time they stopped for lunch, they were surrounded by tall ponderosa pine and juniper.

According to the blacksmith, it was twenty or so miles from Raton's Pass to Colin's ranch. Rafe had hoped to make it before nightfall, but he hadn't counted on the elevation and how it would affect the horses. They'd been accustomed to flat land and now they would be steadily climbing to about four-thousand feet.

"We may have to spend another night," Rafe said while they were eating.

"I think we should push on, Rafe. The horses have new shoes, and this is a good trail."

"And you're ready to sleep in a proper bed," he said teasingly.

"What if they didn't get our letter?" Tom asked.

"I sent one from St. Louis and another one back at the fort," Rafe answered. "They'll be expecting us—you can be sure of that. We've had a couple of delays, so they'll be wondering why we're not there yet."

"Maybe they'll send out a scout," Tom said with excitement.

"You listened to too many of Billy's stories," Rafe said, pulling his son in for a good-natured hug and ruffling his hair.

"Hey, when did you get so tall? You're gonna outgrow me before we get there."

Tom straightened up a little taller. "It's about time," he said. "I'll be fourteen tomorrow."

Rafe looked at Dora. "Is that right? I don't even know what day it is."

"That's right," she said. "He's been countin' the days off by notching them on the wagon. Tomorrow's the tenth day of September." She looked at Tom. "Maybe we can make you a cake when we get to your Uncle Colin's house," she said.

THE SUN WAS LONG GONE but they pushed on until they could no longer see the trail.

"We better stop," Dora said. "The trail's getting narrow and we don't know what lies ahead." She had the reins and she stopped the horses.

Rafe was relieved. "I'll feed the horses, but we'll keep 'em hitched. It can't be too much farther. As soon as it gets daylight we'll light out."

"I'll heat up some coffee, but if it's alright with you, we'll eat dried beef for supper," Dora said. "We won't need much of a fire for coffee. Tom, gather a few sticks, would you?"

She got the coffee grounds and the pot out of the wagon. "Why don't we make room in the wagon for all of us," she said. "It's cold and since we won't be setting up camp and making a fire, we'll all be chilled."

"That suits me," Rafe said. He fed the horses and began to take a few things out of the wagon.

They woke up to the sound of birds and the sun filtering through the pines. Rafe got out first and went to the woods. Tom was right behind him. Dora went to the water barrel and poured water into a pan to freshen up.

"I smell smoke," Tom said, coming out of the woods first.

Dora sniffed the air. "So do I. Someone must be camped nearby. Maybe you should get the gun handy."

Before Tom reached the back of the wagon, Rafe came out of the woods. His eyes were filled with excitement.

"There's a cabin ahead with a big corral and horses," he said.

"Do you think it's Colin's?" Dora asked.

"There's only one way to find out. Get the gear back in the wagon and hop in." He and Tom both ran to the back and loaded up what they took out the night before. Tom jumped in the back and Rafe lifted Dora to the front with one scoop.

"Don't hurry in too fast," she said. "They might think we're somebody up to no good."

"What do you expect me to do, woman? Just stroll in like we're going to a barn dance?"

She laughed and lightly touched the horse's rump with the crop. "Giddyup," she shouted and off they went at a full trot.

THE HORSES SEEMED to be propelled by the same exuberant force and they galloped through the open gate as if St. Peter himself was standing there cheering them on. They had arrived! They had conquered the trail and the two McCade families greeted each other with hugs and back slapping.

Colin pulled his brother aside. "I got your letter from the fort saying you were coming so I got the boys started working on your cabin. Now that you're here, we can finish it. I didn't know how big you would want it in case there's to be more little McCades to make room for."

Rafe smiled, but his brother could see the smile was forced.

"I'm sorry, Rafe. I didn't mean to pry. I remember how broken-hearted Dora was after she lost the baby. I imagine it would be painful to worry about that happening again."

Rafe nodded. "I don't think either of us could go through that pain again. There were many times I wondered if Dora would ever recover and in some ways she never did."

"Does anyone ever recover from losing a child?" Colin asked. "I think a woman takes it harder. It's just built into 'em, you know. They're softer inside."

"I was worried about her for a long time but coming out here has been good for her. She's a little more strong-willed than the Dora I brought home to Kentucky but she's still the same soft-hearted woman inside. I just love her and let her be."

"You're a good man, Rafe. You're the best-hearted of all of us McCades. Don't you worry—we'll get your house done in no time. Meanwhile, you'll stay with us. We've an extra bedroom for you and Dora, and the boys can bunk together." He put his hand on Rafe's shoulder and smiled. "Man, I'm glad you're here! It's a fine thing to have family around. I'd like nothing better than to get Kirk out here too. Wouldn't that be something?"

"He wants to come. Maybe he will after Sarah's ma passes. She's been sickly for a while."

"I went ahead and filed a legal claim for this land," Colin said. "A lot of folks just settle on a piece of land and think that's good enough. They don't count on the greedy nature of people. Me and you—we've been through it first-hand with Aiden.

"We qualified for 640 acres each with the Land Claim Act of 1850, so I filed for that first. Then they were selling it for $1.25 per acre if a person wanted more, so I went ahead and paid the difference for 360 acres for each of us. That gives us both 1000 acres. You can pay me when you're able. Brother Ennis filed for 640 acres. He plans to add to it when he returns from California. He's had some luck mining for gold out there and he's bringing almost a thousand head of cattle with him when he comes back."

"I can pay you soon," Rafe said. "And I should have some extra to start a small herd for myself."

At Colin's questioning look, he grinned. "The US marshal out of Santa Fe will be bringing us some money in a week or two." He went on to tell Colin about the two men they'd tied up back in the desert.

Colin shook his head when Rafe finished the story. "That girl's full of spunk; I'll give her that."

"You don't know the half of it," Rafe said, taking his hat off and shaking the dust out of it. "I imagine Dora McCade stories are being told from here to Kentucky by now."

"I can't wait to hear them all."

Rafe thought about that. It would be a while before he could tell his brother he'd had to kill a man. But he would in time.

Tom and young Lenny walked around the corner. "So, this is Tom? He wasn't much bigger than Lenny here when we left Kentucky."

"He turns fourteen today," Rafe said. "He's almost as tall as me."

Colin put his arm across Tom's shoulder. "Out here, a boy fifteen is considered a man if he's up for it. You'll be a good hand to have around." With his arm still on Tom's shoulder, he started walking. "Let's take a quick look at the barn and then we'll go back in the house. Mira will have started breakfast by now. I know you boys are hungry."

"That we are," Rafe said. "We rode so hard yesterday, we were too tired to build much of a fire when we stopped. Cold biscuits and jerky don't hold a man over for long."

COLIN'S WIFE, Mira, was of German descent and her rosy cheeks and easy smile made Dora feel welcome. She was holding a chubby baby boy in her arms and it was easy to see he was a McCade. Mira's older son was Lenny. His hair was the color of straw and Dora figured him to be about seven. He and Tom walked away following after the men.

"Come on in the house, Dora," Mira said. "You look fresh as a daisy. You must not have traveled far this morning."

"I'm far from fresh, Mira. We came a long way yesterday and I'm worn plumb out. If we'd known we were so close, we would have come on in last night."

"Well, you're here now and that's all that matters. I'm thankful to have a woman to share things with. As you can see, I'm surrounded by boys." She bounced the baby in her arms, and he laughed. "I was thinking this one would have been a girl, but the good Lord must have known that Colin needed another boy for the ranch."

"He's a handsome baby," Dora said. "What's his name?"

"I wanted to name him after his Pa, but Colin wanted to name him Benjamin. We call him Ben."

"That was Papa McCade's name," Dora said. "It's nice you named him after his grandpa." Her eyes grew misty. "Tom's named after my pa, and the baby girl we lost, Alice, she was named after my ma." She gave a big sigh. "I wonder…"

Mira's face was full of sympathy. "Colin told me you had lost a child. I'm so sorry."

Dora brushed a tear aside and gave a half-smile. "Can I help you with breakfast, Mira? I smelled bacon when I walked in."

"You're all hungry no doubt. I've made bacon and biscuits already and was just peeling potatoes when we heard your wagon. Watch the baby and I'll finish peeling the potatoes and fry 'em up."

"Ah," Dora said, taking the baby from her. "I don't mind a bit." Holding Ben in her arms, she looked around the room. Colin's skill as a craftsman stood out in this house he had built of logs from their ranch with only an adze and a broadax for tools. She admired how the logs had been chinked together for a tight fit in order to hold the cold weather at bay during the harsh winter months. The kitchen area held a wood cooking stove, a rustic table with benches, and a hanging rack for pots and pans. A quilt was draped over a long bench in the living area and several rocking chairs were lined up facing the fireplace. A big fire was blazing, and it felt good. She was still chilled from being outside, so she sat down with the baby in one of the rockers in front of the fire. Ben looked her over and decided she was safe, so he settled his head on her shoulder and started sucking his thumb.

She nuzzled his soft baby cheeks with her own and breathed in the sweet baby scent. As he lay against her, she felt a firm thump from her midsection. She had held the secret close to her heart long enough now. She counted back the weeks since she'd noticed the first early signs of pregnancy. It had been mid-May and here it was mid-September. She was now noticeably plumper, and she wondered if Rafe had noticed.

Mira was humming a German tune as she worked in the kitchen, and Dora rocked back and forth, enjoying the warmth of the fireplace and the baby against her breast. She smiled as she thought of how she would tell Rafe tonight. Ranch life would be hard, but what a fine place to raise a family! As she thought it all out, she still ached inside for the babies she'd lost, and her hand automatically reached for the locket she wore around her neck. Alice would always hold a special place in her heart, but oh how grateful she was for another chance.

The fire blazed brightly as Mira added another log to the fireplace, but Dora didn't notice. Her heart was content as she dozed in the rocking chair with the sweet assurance of God's loving grace.

The End

NOTES

CHAPTER 2

1. HMdb.org Historical Marker Data Base, Site of Starns' Defeat

CHAPTER 4

1. *TrueWest Magazine,* Shootin' Shot, March 2005 Edition S

OTHER BOOKS BY GLENDA MANUS

The Southern Grace Series

Book 1 - Sweet Tea and Southern Grace

Book 2 - Lighting the Way

Book 3 - High Tide at Pelican Pointe

Book 4 - The Melancholy Moon

Book 5 - The Sweet Tea Quilting Bee

Book 6 - Miss Marple's B&B

Book 7 – Finding Maisy

Book 8 – Home to Park Place

(More to come)

∾

Western Historical Fiction

Book 1 - Follow the Westward Star

AUTHOR'S NOTE

Thank you for reading **Follow the Westward Star.** *Although it is quite a change from the cozy mysteries I've written before, it's been fun to branch out and try something new. I will return to the Southern Grace Series with my next book, so keep watching for new releases.*

Although trials and tribulations follow Dora and Rafe as they venture westward in this book, God's loving grace shines through. My prayer is that you too will be touched by grace as you read Follow the Westward Star.

I love hearing from you, and if you've enjoyed reading this or any of my books, I hope you'll leave a review on Amazon and Goodreads. You may also connect with me on my Facebook page, **Glenda C MANUS***, with my last name* **all in caps***. On that page, I give periodic updates of books I'm working on and I try to add some inspirational messages. I can also be contacted by email at gecm1948@gmail.com.*

Happy Reading!

Glenda Manus